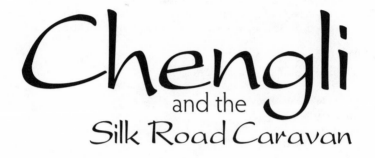

Chengli
and the
Silk Road Caravan

Hildi Kang

Tanglewood • Terre Haute, IN

Published by Tanglewood Publishing, Inc., October 2011.

Design by Amy Alick Perich
Cover illustration by Marcy Jean Stacey

Tanglewood Publishing, Inc.
P. O. Box 3009
Terre Haute, IN 47803
www.tanglewoodbooks.com

Printed in by Maple Vail Press, York, PA, USA.
10 9 8 7 6 5 4 3 2 1

ISBN 978-1-933718-54-5

Library of Congress Cataloging-in-Publication Data

Kang, Hildi, 1934-
  Chengli and the Silk Road caravan / by Hildi Kang.
     p. cm.
  Summary: Called to follow the wind and search for information about his father who disappeared many years ago, thirteen-year-old Chengli, carrying a piece of jade with strange writing that had belonged to his father, joins a caravan charged with giving safe passage to the Emperor's daughter as it navigates the constant dangers of the Silk Road in 630 A.D.
  ISBN 978-1-933718-54-5
  [1. Silk Road--Fiction. 2. Caravans--Fiction. 3. Trade routes--Fiction. 4. China--History--221 B.C.-960 A.D.--Fiction. 5. Princesses--Fiction. 6. Fathers--Fiction.] I. Title.
  PZ7.K12764Che 2011
  [Fic]--dc22
                              2010047359

one

Chang'an, China's Imperial City, 630 CE

IT WAS THE WIND THAT MADE CHENGLI DECIDE TO LEAVE. Yellow with dust from the desert, it rolled and danced around his ears during the day and pounded black against his eyes in the night. A demon wind, it taunted him to remember places long forgotten. A spirit wind, it teased him to recall events he had never known.

Yet as he guided his donkey cart through the crowded streets of Chang'an city, no wind blew. The golden banners that marked the Chinese emperor's palace lay limp against their poles. Along the canal, the leaves on the willow trees hung motionless in the spring sunshine.

"Can't you hear it? Don't you feel it?" Chengli called to his partner riding along with him in the cart.

"You know, don't you—there is no wind!" Little Limp shouted as he sat at the back of the cart, protecting the bolts of silk and guarding his injured foot, the one that refused to heal properly. As long as Chengli could remember, he and Little Limp had worked together for the silk merchant. When they were children, they'd been given easy jobs, for the merchant said if they wanted to eat, they had to work.

1

When they were five or six, they used short, stubby brooms and swept out the stinking animal droppings from the stalls of the two donkeys until their arms ached so much they could barely lift the chopsticks to eat their rice. As they grew older and stronger, they exchanged the brooms for shovels to rid the stalls of rotten straw. Now that they were twelve and thirteen and tall for their ages, the merchant trusted them to work together on the delivery cart, going back and forth daily across the great city.

Little Limp pulled himself up to look over the piles of silk and to face Chengli. "You know, nobody else feels the wind. It's a ghost wind, and it doesn't want me; it only wants you."

Chengli jammed his fists against his ears to block out the sound of the wind. "It's driving me crazy!"

"Maybe it's not wind at all," said Little Limp, spreading his fingers and waving his arms wildly. "It's *demon* breath! Eiiiii!" he yelled in his best demon voice. "It's a desert demon from the far, far north. Maybe it's trying to pull you back there. Isn't that where you were born? Isn't that where your father died? Maybe the demons know something. Maybe . . ." Little Limp's voice trailed off as Chengli leaped up and pounded the air.

"Aiii! Demon from the desert," Chengli shouted, "show yourself! Let me fight you fair and square!"

Little Limp grinned. He was used to his older friend's bursts of temper, especially when things didn't seem right. And a demon that hid in the wind was not right—not at all. "You can't fight the wind," he called to Chengli.

Chengli relaxed, gave his donkey a swat, and thought about what Little Limp had said. A demon wind calling him to the desert? That couldn't be right. He planned to stay right where he was. He loved this imperial city of Chang'an, all laid out in its perfect square, with the main streets going straight across in each direction and leading to the gate in each of the four walls. Off the busy main streets, smaller streets and alleys twisted and curved, and Chengli knew every one of them. He knew the filthy alleys to the south and the elegant, stone-paved streets surrounding the emperor's palace near the north wall. He watched for a glimpse of the emperor, or even a prince or princess, but he'd never seen them. Instead he gave his attention to the silk that he delivered, the cart that carried it, even the old donkey that pulled the cart. Little Limp was smart enough for a young kid, thought Chengli, but he must be wrong about that horrible wind. Yet maybe . . .

Chengli thought about all the years he and Little Limp had worked together for bald-headed Merchant Yan, the wealthiest silk merchant in the city. He thought about all the talk he heard as he walked back and forth through the city. Men spoke of how this year, the fifth year in the reign of the Emperor Taizong, promised to be a good year for merchants. And if it was good for merchants, it would be good for the caravans carrying their wares. "Maybe," Chengli said out loud, "maybe it's time I left this city to follow the spirit wind, so I can find out what it wants from me."

They passed through the opening in the wall that surrounded the vast East Market and made their way through the familiar puzzle of narrow alleys, past small shops selling everything from salt to timber, from precious jewels to horses, and one—Chengli's favorite—that sold twenty-four different kinds of dumplings. He urged his donkey around the mats laid out on the ground on which peddlers had set out their wares. When the two boys reached the stalls that clustered together in the street where fabrics were sold, they delivered the bolts of silk to those merchants who had the emperor's permission to sell the precious material, and then they headed for their last delivery of the day, at a caravan parked in the field outside the high stone wall of the city.

Chengli climbed up on Old Donkey's bare back, and he guided the cart along dusty streets, past the bell tower with its huge bronze bell that rang the curfew at night and the opening of the city gates in the morning. They continued across town past the drum tower and then, nodding to the soldier on duty, out through the archway in the massive, red-brick gate to the grassy field where the caravans gathered.

Everywhere across the field, the rugged men who worked the caravans had pitched their small tents or thrown their blanket rolls down on the ground to claim their spots. They had tethered their camels and donkeys and now stood arguing and bargaining in a confusion of sounds and smells, voices, snorts, and bellows. Soon these men would load their string of camels with thousands of precious items and begin the long trek to the northwest along the route used by the huge trade caravans. Out there somewhere, they would leave the protection of China's Great Wall and head west around the edge of the fearful desert until they reached a city called Kashgar.

That's the place, Chengli had heard, where hundreds of caravans from far distant lands came together to buy and sell everything, exchanging their loads for new things and then turning around and returning the way they had come. The caravan men told him nothing about the far lands, for they'd never been there and didn't believe the stories they were told. The mountains blocking the way north, west, and south were so high and cold that no camel could cross them, and only magical horses brought loads down out of the snow. Such lands, Chengli knew, were protected by ghosts and demons and dragons—not the friendly river dragons of the Middle Kingdom, but ferocious dragons of the sand and snow. And the men told of the demons in the billowing clouds that hung over the highest mountains, often pushing their clouds down so low that whole caravans fell over the cliffs into the chasms below. Only the bravest men could face such unknown terrors.

Moving on through the crowded field, Chengli wrinkled his nose against the overwhelming stench of so many camels, while his slender body bounced to the rhythmic rustle of bells and bangles that hung from the camels' saddles. Men yelled, camels hummed, ropes slapped, and workers adjusted their loads of silk, spices, tea, and pottery to take to the lands beyond the mountains.

Chengli worked his way across the field until he saw the blue-and-white banner that identified his assigned caravan master and brought his cart to a stop. Little Limp jumped down off the back of the cart, lost his balance, and fell to the ground at the feet of the master. Chengli leaped off the donkey and dropped to his hands and knees next to his partner in respect for the caravan master.

"Stand!" the man ordered. "What have you brought me?"

Chengli held out a thin, wooden paddle covered with writing: the record of silk to be delivered. As workers unloaded the heavy rolls of fabric, the master checked each bolt for the imperial seal that marked it as having been inspected and approved for sale.

"Fifty bolts of plain white silk," counted the caravan master, "and fifty bolts of silk woven in colorful patterns approved for trade."

Satisfied, he recorded the delivery on the wooden paddle and handed it back. Chengli took the paddle, slipped it under the rope that served as his belt, and tied it securely. He pulled his rough, brown tunic tighter over his shoulders and, with a yank at Old Donkey's rope, turned back toward the city.

Leading the donkey through the crowded streets of Chang'an, he jostled against the people and animals that filled every available space. Street cleaners and peddlers shoved aside cows, cats, and children as they wandered in all directions. Porters carried their wares on wooden yokes across their shoulders, and thin old men in long, tattered robes coughed a constant "Move! Move!" to their heavily loaded mules. The enticing aromas of soup and spices twisted in and out among the sharper smells of people and animals, body sweat and manure.

People came to Chang'an from every far-away place— countries from beyond those magical clouds that hid the mountains beyond the desert—to trade with the Middle Kingdom. The people who came to Chang'an looked different and sounded different. They came with black hair, red hair, curly hair, long beards, no beards, brown eyes, blue eyes. None of them pulled their hair up into topknots the way all the Middle Kingdom people did . . . all except Chengli, of course, as his hair had been shaved off by Old Cook, and it was just growing long again. He didn't like to talk about that.

He did, however, like to watch the foreigners. They talked with words strange to the ear and ate foods strange in taste and smell. Chengli loved this part of the city, the Western Market, and he always slowed the cart to look at the silver and gold jewelry, and the woven straw baskets filled with dried fish and a smell so strong it made Chengli's nose crinkle long before he even got near them. He listened to the women bargaining to get the cheapest price, watched the herb seller mix medicines with strange-sounding names, and stopped to gaze at the piles of vegetables he knew and those he feared even to touch. But today the sights and sounds made him feel restless.

"I've worked these streets every day of my life for the past four years," Chengli said to Little Limp, who was sitting behind him in the now-empty cart. "It's the only home I know, but I think you are right. The desert is calling me. I was born out there somewhere, you know, where the grass and trees disappear and nothing is left except rock and sand and mountains. I've heard about it forever from Old Cook, because she still tells me stories my mother once told her. And now I want to see it. I'm old enough to work in one of the caravans heading out along the trade route. With them I can travel in safety."

"Caravans don't need skinny boys, they need men," Little Limp teased. "You'll have to fight bandits—*real* bandits. And

ghosts as thick as desert sands." He shivered and put his
hands over his eyes. "And there are demons out there—real
ones—prowling along the tops of the mountains and sliding
down through the clouds to catch careless travelers. I've heard
people say the trails along the edge of the desert are lined
with bones of people eaten by those hungry, desert spirits."

Chengli's voice tightened. "Maybe you're right," he said.
"I am skinny, but I'm tall and I'm strong. And don't you
notice? Caravans come and go all the time. Most people
survive . . . even if my own parents didn't."

"If your father died out there," Little Limp said, "Old
Cook must know where he is buried."

"Old Cook doesn't know. Maybe my father never *was*
buried."

"Then maybe he never really died."

"What do you mean?" Chengli asked. "Old Cook says
he died. Bandits came. Father disappeared. And, Cook says,
the bandits always kill their prisoners."

"Do you remember your father at all?"

"No. But lately I've been thinking about him," Chengli
said as he ran his hands through his tousled hair and gazed
off into the distance. "I know he worked as one of the
inspector generals for the government, checking the packs
that the caravans bring in and out of our land. Making sure
they have the correct passport. Making sure they carry just
what their documents listed and nothing more. Old Cook
says Father was brave and honest—he never lied and he
never took bribes."

Chengli turned the cart toward their home and
continued, "I have no idea what he was really like, and the

older I get, the more I wonder. The only thing I do know is that in order for him to become an inspector, he had to pass the government exam, and to do that, he had to know how to read and write. His family must have been rich to pay for his teacher. So I know he wasn't a low-class serf, a servant like me. But I don't know anything else at all about him. I do wonder what he was like. Am I like my father? I'll never know. But maybe somebody out there knew him. Maybe somebody can tell me more about him."

Little Limp scooted forward in the empty cart. "How did you get *here*, if you were born out *there*?"

"The story Old Cook tells is that when Mother got sick, she managed to join a caravan so she could bring me back to our city, Chang'an. She gave me to Old Cook. And then she died." Chengli shook his head, lost in his own thoughts.

He guided the cart around a fountain and over the great stone bridge, until they finally reached the high stone walls of Merchant Yan's house. They passed the main entrance with its heavily carved wooden doors and pushed open the smaller gate that led to the servants' area. A long corridor led to an open courtyard, where along the outer wall stood the rooms to house the servants, animals, storage, and tools. They stopped at the stalls for their donkey and cart. Little Limp jumped down and unhitched Old Donkey.

"People say—" Little Limp began.

"I don't care what people say. I want to join a caravan!" Chengli grabbed a handful of straw and scraped at the donkey's back and sides to clean off the dust of the city, until the old animal pulled away from such rough treatment. Wrinkling his brow in thought, Chengli dropped the straw.

"I was born in the year of the *tiger*! I must be as fierce and strong as tigers."

Little Limp looked puzzled. "How will you get free from your contract to work for Merchant Yan?" he asked. "He won't want to lose such cheap labor. It doesn't cost him much to feed kids like us."

"I won't even try," Chengli said. "I'll just leave." He headed off across the courtyard to the building that served as a kitchen for all the servants. But as he walked, he thought about Old Cook, and he knew he could not leave without telling her. She had cared for him all these years, and he owed her honor and respect. She was the only person who really cared about him at all, and he must tell her about his plans. His thoughts flew this way and that way, searching for the best way to tell her.

He walked to the door of the kitchen and stopped. The aroma of sweet, cooked rice filled the dingy, dirt-floor room, blending with the savory smell of sizzling onions. Chengli always thought that frying onions must be the most delicious smell in the world, and it usually made him stop at the doorway and give the proper greeting, "I have returned, Honorable Auntie," followed by "Something sure smells good in here!"

Tonight, however, he stood silently in the shadows and watched as Old Cook bent low, pushing branches into the opening of the stone fire-bench. She was more like a mother to him, scolding or chiding him when he needed it, listening quietly when he had fits of anger or sadness, or caring for him when he got sick. So he knew that if he really wanted to leave Chang'an, he had to start here. He blinked his large brown eyes, sucked in a quick breath, let it out slowly, and stepped out of the shadows.

"Well," Old Cook said, looking up with a toothless grin, "you are quiet tonight. What's on your mind, young one?"

"Auntie, I have to tell you something." Chengli walked around to where the old woman, her skin thinner than wrinkled rice paper, expertly ladled steaming food from a large, black kettle into a row of bowls lined up on the serving board. "Today I watched caravans prepare to leave Chang'an." He dug his toes into the dirt floor and tried again. "I want to go with them."

Old Cook kept ladling out rice with one hand and brushed the sweat off her face with the other. "You've said that every autumn and every spring since you've been old enough to talk."

Chengli gulped for air and talked faster. "Auntie, somewhere in my mind there are bits and pieces of another life, of horses and camels, heat and wind. I am now in my thirteenth year, old enough to go find that life."

Old Cook looked up and stared at him. "You? Go into the desert? Huh! Demons will eat you in one bite." The old woman cackled at her own joke.

"Demons don't eat caravan men, and they won't eat me."

"Men? You're young and soft, just right for demon food. And if those spirits don't get you, the wild winds will blow you away. The winds will tear you into shreds and float you back to me in little specks of yellow dust." The woman turned again to the rice pot, shivering at her thoughts of unknown terrors.

Chengli swallowed hard. He really hadn't seen a caravan

worker as young as he, but he wasn't going to let Old Cook discourage him. She got scared just peeking at the streets outside her own gate.

A heavy silence stretched to fill the room. Then, slowly, Cook turned from the stove to face Chengli. "Your poor mother gave you to me. She begged me to raise you as my own son. I promised her. I promised her when she lay dying," her voice shrilled. "What are you saying? That I break a deathbed promise? All the ghosts of all the dead in the Middle Kingdom will come and steal my spirit if I break my promise!"

Chengli clenched his fists to help him keep his mouth shut and nodded his thanks for his rice bowl. He sat down on the bench and watched the other workers come in for their suppers. Eating slowly, he finished his rice and then walked back across the room to stand near Old Cook. His words were ready now.

"Auntie, you've already done what my mother asked. You are a mother to me. You've cared for me all these years. But I don't have to *live* here. The ghost wind is making me crazy! I have to go with the caravans and chase that wind to see if my memories are real. And maybe," he hesitated, "maybe I'll even find someone who can tell me about my father."

"Your father?" Old Cook swung around and grabbed Chengli by the shoulders, shaking him. "I've told you a million times! Bandits killed your father. Do you want bandits to kill you, too?"

Chengli's head bobbed wildly and his unruly shaggy hair flopped into his eyes as Old Cook took out her fear on his body. Now he knew for sure that she loved him like a real mother, but he had to finish what he had started.

"Not everybody gets killed by bandits!" He brushed the hair off his face and flung his arms out wide. "People come this way and go that way and come and go, again and again. I know it. I see them—the same people—when I take the silk out to the caravans. I *will* come back. I'll come back and tell you about all the strange and marvelous things that I've seen."

"Go then, you ungrateful mutt. Go right now!" Old Cook grabbed a piece of firewood and turned toward him, beating at the air. Chengli dropped his rice bowl and ducked outside, grinning right down to his toes. He had the permission he needed.

two

EARLY THE NEXT MORNING, while the other servants still snuffled and snored in their sleep, Chengli rose in silence from his raised, brick sleeping bench, gathered up his blanket and his extra pair of baggy brown pants, and slipped from the room. This morning he would go take a closer look at those caravans and choose one to join.

In the pre-dawn darkness, he made his way through the courtyard-house, along the path that separated the two main courtyards from those of the servants, and then carefully walked around the ornately carved, wooden screen that guarded the front entrance from evil spirits. He lifted the bolt in the gate, willing it not to creak, and stepped outside. He'd gone down this alley many times, but this time he had no donkey, no cart, and no Little Limp. What he did have was a tight knot in the pit of his stomach. He stepped away from the only life he'd ever known.

He walked to the main road and headed toward the dark silhouette of the city gate. He'd never seen it in the dark of early morning, and he stared up at the top where the wide eaves of the lookout tower's roof curved skyward like some huge bird spreading its wings. Standing there, he waited with the others until the bronze bell in the center of the city rang out to announce the opening of the gates. The soldier in the watchtower called in his loud voice, "All is well! Chang'an greets a new day!"

Hearing the call, the soldiers on guard lifted the huge, oaken beam and shoved apart the massive wooden doors. As the gates groaned open, crowds of people crushed through to begin their day. Those waiting outside pushed in, and those waiting inside shoved their way out. Chengli elbowed his way into a space behind a rumbling ox cart, moved out through the gate, and headed to the nearby field where the caravans were parked.

The morning mist lay close to the ground, waiting for the rising sun to burn it away. Everywhere he looked, animals lay resting like gray-brown boulders. Scattered among them stood the men, stretching, yawning, and folding up their blankets. Thin wisps of smoke rose from fires where cooks prepared breakfast. Which one shall I approach? wondered Chengli. What will I say?

"Hey, boy! What brings you out here so early?" a voice challenged him.

Startled, Chengli turned. A boy, head and shoulders taller than he and dressed in the short, brown tunic and baggy, gray pants of the caravan trade, came up behind him.

"I've seen you before. Where's your donkey cart?" the boy asked with an easy smile that invited confidence.

"Didn't bring it," Chengli answered. "I'm coming to work on a caravan."

"Who're you working for?" the older boy asked.

"Don't know. Don't have a job yet."

"Then it's a good thing I found you, boy. I have the perfect job for you. With a good master. Come on."

Curious, Chengli fell into step beside the new boy. "Who are you?" he asked, cautious of such an easy friendship.

"They call me Fourth Brother," said the boy. "My family is large, and my father gave me to the caravan master so that I'd have food to eat. Master Fong, the leader of our caravan, says I'm strong enough now to work with the caravan guards instead of the animals." The boy clenched his fists and flexed his arm muscles right in front of Chengli's face. "That means, you see, they'll need somebody to take over my old job."

"What did you do?" asked Chengli.

"A bunch of the easy jobs: help the cook, take care of the camels and donkeys . . . lots of things."

Chengli opened his mouth to ask what "lots" really meant, but the boy stopped beside a man bending over the side of a resting camel, mending the tears in a red-and-black blanket that fit around the beast's two humps.

"Master Fong," said Fourth Brother, "I've brought you a new worker." The boy bowed to his master and then ducked around to the other side of the camel and tugged on the ropes to secure the blanket.

Master Fong looked up and Chengli jumped back, startled at the fierce expression on the man's face. "Who? Where?" he asked, ignoring Chengli. Thick black eyebrows shadowed the man's eyes, and a frown deepened the lines of his wrinkled face. A scar across his left cheek gave evidence of a fight.

"Me, Honorable Master," Chengli said. "I've come to work for you."

"You?" The master spat on the ground. "You are a child. We have no work for children."

Chengli felt his mouth drop open—he might be small, but he was <u>not</u> a child. "I'm not a child! I'm thirteen and I'm strong." He pulled up straighter, trying to look sturdier, and in doing so, he forgot to show respect to the older man. He took a deep breath and began again.

"Sir, my family name is Chao. My personal name is Chengli. I am the son of Imperial Inspector Chao Changwon. I know I'm skinny, but I've worked for the silk merchant since I was six years old. And," he said, his eyes flashing, "I can work for you."

The man looked up and exploded into laughter. "Ha!" he roared. "Whoever you are, you are one determined tadpole— but still too young to work a caravan! Can you ride? Can you bargain? Can you fight? I think not! Be gone!" The man turned his back on Chengli and continued his work.

Chengli's face tensed, and his ears burned as he concentrated on this new insult. Forcing himself to think slowly, he remembered his manners, bowed his head, and looked down at the ground.

"Good Master, may you live forever! I am young and truly of no account," he said, "but I *can* work hard."

"You are too young—and I see you have a bit of a temper. Not good for the caravan. Go away."

Chengli stepped back, blew out a great puff of air, and tried to think what to do next. Before he could speak, a new sound cut through the morning air.

"Make way! Make way for the Words of the Emperor!"

Across the field marched four men, dressed in the long, red robes that marked them as imperial messengers. A servant in front, holding aloft the red, silk banner embroidered with a golden dragon, called out the warning. Each man walked with his head held high, his mouth tight, and his eyes staring straight ahead. Chengli thought they looked as though they were trying to pinch the unwelcome smell of camels, horses, and donkeys out of their important imperial noses.

"Master Fong!" the flag bearer bellowed. "We seek Master Fong!"

Master's face drained of color. His scowl disappeared. He dropped to his knees as he called out, "At your service, Most Honorable Excellency." Chengli stopped staring and dropped to all fours beside the master.

"Master Fong, the records say that you are officially licensed to carry silk to the far kingdom of Kashgar. Is that true?"

"Yes, my lord."

"You have made this journey many times—all successfully?"

"Yes, my lord."

"Our Great and Glorious Emperor knows of your record and chooses you for a high honor. He sends a princess, the Princess Meiling, to marry King Galdan, ruler of a nomad kingdom in the great mountains north of Kashgar. The princess, with her possessions and personal servants, will join you tomorrow. The journey of over two thousand miles is full of danger. For her safety, she will travel in the middle of your caravan. She will be protected by her own royal guards—with the assistance of your men."

Master Fong bent low, shoving his forehead deeper into the dust. "I am not worthy of such an honor," he grumbled.

Behind him, Chengli caught the whisper of Fourth Brother's voice. "He isn't prepared for it, either."

As if in echo, Master Fong continued, "I am ill prepared for such an honor, my lord. My workers are clumsy and ignorant men."

"And he doesn't want to wait until tomorrow to start," came the whisper from behind the camel's hump. "He's ready to leave today."

The messenger stepped forward and handed Master Fong a wooden document covered with writing. "The princess and her carts will arrive at sun-up tomorrow. Here are your orders. She is to be delivered to the fair-haired King Galdan, who will meet your caravan when it reaches the oasis of Kashgar at the end of the great Taklamakan Desert. Her servants will travel with you and then accompany her to her new home. His Majesty has spoken."

The men did not wait for an answer. They turned away, and with robes billowing, feet marching, and eyes staring straight ahead, they followed their flag bearer back toward the safety of the city.

"Well, Tadpole." Master Fong's rough voice made Chengli scramble to his feet. "I see you are still here. Now it appears you can be useful after all. Fourth Brother," Master said, motioning to the older boy, "you and the skinny one, go tell the others who plan to travel with us that we are delayed until tomorrow. They will understand. They have seen the messengers."

Fourth Brother and Chengli ran off in opposite directions to deliver the message to each caravan master. When Chengli finished and turned back toward Master Fong, he noticed a small boy with a lopsided limp coming across the field.

"Little Limp? What are you doing out here?" Chengli yelled and then stopped in surprise as he saw Fourth Brother run up behind the boy, knock him down, and keep on running.

"Stop, thief!" Little Limp yelled, scrambling to his feet and pointing after Fourth Brother.

Chengli propelled his body forward, dodged around loaded camels, and sprinted across the field. He collided with Fourth Brother, throwing him off balance and slamming him to the ground.

"Let go of me!" yelled Fourth Brother.

"What did you steal?"

"Nothing! You're crazy! I have nothing!"

"Liar!" Little Limp called out. "He's got the packet! Old Cook sent me to find you. She said to give it to *you*."

Chengli straddled Fourth Brother and pounded on his back. The bigger boy yelled and squirmed, but Chengli held him down. "Well?" he barked to the back of Fourth Brother's head.

"Oh, this? How was I supposed to know it was yours?" Fourth Brother opened his hand. A small, brown bundle of rough cloth tumbled out. "You're my friend. I'd never lay a hand on anything of yours. Here, take it."

Chengli grabbed the packet and wondered how he'd suddenly become Fourth Brother's friend.

"Open it. Let's see what you have," Fourth Brother grinned as he rolled over to sit on the ground. "Don't look so worried. I won't touch it. I'm your friend, remember?"

Chengli unfolded the cloth. Into his hand slid a crescent of pale green jade, broken along one edge, with part of a word written in unfamiliar script etched across the surface. He rubbed his finger over the writing, wondering what it said.

"Ho! Now who's the thief?" Fourth Brother leaned forward to stare at the stone in Chengli's hand. "There's no way a servant boy owns *that*!"

Chengli held the precious jade in his hand. "I didn't steal it. It belonged to my father. Old Cook told me about it, but I've never seen it before." He stared at the jade, turned it over, smelled it, and then rubbed it slowly against his cheek. Wherever the jade touched, he felt the coolness of a soft spring breeze.

Little Limp, coming near now that it seemed safe, pulled at Chengli's tunic to get his attention. "Old Cook said that this piece of jade should unlock the secrets of your past. News of your father—and your own future—might be hidden with the other half of this jade. If you can find the broken piece, the person who has it may know the answers . . . and maybe then," Little Limp paused and shrugged his shoulders, "the wind will finally let go of you."

"I've seen jade like that at the bazaar," Fourth Brother said in awe, still gawking at the precious stone, "but I've never touched it."

"Here," Chengli said, "feel it." He watched the older boy run his fingers across the smooth surface and touch them carefully along the jagged, broken edge. Then Chengli took the stone, put it into the small cloth pouch tied to his belt, and pulled the string tight.

Chengli closed his hand firmly over the packet that now hung at his side. "I've never touched anything that belonged to my father," he murmured, wondering why the jade was broken. What had happened to the rest of it?

He stood there on the field, his mind full of questions, pondering what to do next. Master Fong had told him to go spread the news of the caravan's delay, and he'd done that. Did that mean he was hired? The only way to find out was to go back to the master and ask him.

As he approached, the master looked up. His gruff voice made Chengli wince. "I see that you fight easily. Are you a quarrelsome lad?" The scar on his face deepened, and Chengli wondered about his own fight.

Chengli remembered his manners. "I am not quarrelsome, Master, but I don't like it when people are unfair or unjust."

"I run an honest caravan," said Master Fong. "We will have no fights—among ourselves, that is. But *work* we will have aplenty."

"Master," said Chengli, remembering his manners, "I am a very worthless person, but I do know how to work. I know how to care for donkeys. I feed them, brush them, clean their hooves, and put ointment on their sores. I know how to soothe their cranky spirits and convince them to work."

"We do have donkeys, but mostly we have camels. Have you ever worked with camels? I think not." The master glanced at the nearest beast, which stared back through long, black eyelashes. "Camels listen, but they do not like to obey orders. When they are well-treated, they are patient, faithful workers, but if not, they bite, they kick, they spit."

"Master, I know nothing about camels, but I am ready to learn."

"You will tire of them, working with them day and night, month after month, perhaps year upon year. It is a long, long walk to Kashgar." Master rubbed his scarred cheek and watched Chengli to see how he would react.

Chengli felt his eyes narrowing and his teeth clenching in frustration. He lowered his head, hoping he looked more respectful than he felt.

"What's a young one like you want on a caravan, anyway? You're better off here in Chang'an. Are you running away? Are you in trouble?" Master Fong's eyes nearly disappeared as his bushy eyebrows pulled down in a menacing frown.

"No, Master, not at all, Master." And Chengli began his story again. "I was born somewhere in the desert; I don't really know where. And now every day and every night I feel the wind. Nobody else feels it. It's desert wind, it's pulling me, and . . ." Chengli stopped and thought of the broken jade. He didn't want to talk about that. He looked back at Master Fong. "I want to go and see the land where I was born."

The master relaxed and his voice softened. "You tell me your name is Chengli, but I will call you as I see you, Skinny One. We can indeed use your hands. Many small caravans will join with our large one, for there is safety in numbers, and now that the princess is also coming with us, we do need workers. I tell you, though—be warned: the desert is more brutal than any human master. Without fail, we will know hunger, thirst, and constant danger. Back out now if you wish."

He waited.

Chengli did not move.

☰

three

"THREE WEEKS ALREADY," CHENGLI MUTTERED. "Three weeks on the road. Sore feet, sore arms—all just as Master Fong said!" Chengli shuffled along beside the camels, trudging north toward the great Huang He, the Yellow River just beyond the city of Lanzhou. Hour after hour, it was all the same. They passed small villages surrounded by patchworks of vegetable gardens and tiny paddies where barefoot farmers bent low planting rice seedlings. In the larger fields, sometimes a farmer could be seen walking behind his ox as they turned over the soil, preparing to plant some new crop. The caravan did not stop at these villages but moved forward at the slow speed of plodding camels.

Chengli's feet hurt, and he thought back wistfully to the comfort of the creaky, rickety cart he had shared with Little Limp. Yet he dared not complain, or Master Fong would just dump him along the side of the road.

Indeed, the work was harder than he'd imagined: taking the loads off the camels at night, loading them up again every morning, tightening ropes, and—the worst part—the walking, walking, walking. He hadn't thought about the endless walking!

And now this.

"Rain, rain, and more rain," he complained to himself as he sloshed along the muddy road beside El Kalid, his lead camel. He pulled down his wide-brimmed straw hat tighter on his head, tipping it forward to keep the rain out of his eyes. His water-soaked clothes stuck to his body, making it even harder to walk.

The rain fell steadily, yellow with grit and heavy with dust blown from the northern deserts. Chengli pulled his hat down farther.

His legs ached from trudging through the mud, his arms ached from pulling on the rope to keep the camels moving, and his hands burned from constantly tightening the rain-slackened ropes to keep the heavy loads in place. He moved back along the line of camels assigned to his care, checking each load until he came to Fourth Brother, who was checking on his own assigned animals, the donkeys.

"I hate these donkeys!" Fourth Brother growled. "Master Fong promised me I could be a guard, but now he has shoved me back with animals. 'That's where you're needed,' he says. I'll show him I can do more than watch over a bunch of lazy donkeys!"

A shrill feminine voice sliced through Fourth Brother's mumbling. "This road is too bumpy! Amah, bring me another pillow. I am cold and wet and this cart leaks. It is a royal cart. It should not leak! Do something!"

"That's the other problem," Fourth Brother added, cocking his head toward the cart behind them. "If I worked as a guard, I could get away from that annoying voice!"

Chengli turned to stare at the covered cart painted with the imperial red and gold that bumped and rumbled behind them. "Who would want to marry a princess with a voice like that?" he muttered, agreeing with Fourth Brother. "All she does is whine."

"I think Master put us here just because we are young and don't dare argue," Fourth Brother grumbled. "The older men refuse to work near that voice."

Chengli looked back again at the royal cart and its driver, who sat huddled under a small red-and-gold umbrella. Next to the cart rode the royal soldiers, each sitting straight and tall and trying to look important as the wind whipped the rain into their faces and the water ran in little rivers down the length of their straw rain coats. Chengli faced into the wind, thankful that this wind was not his demon. This wind tormented everyone.

"Those men must be deaf, listening to her all the time," Fourth Brother added. "I wonder what she looks like. With a voice like that, she must be really ugly. Have you seen her?"

"I don't *want* to see her. Ever!" Chengli yanked at a frayed rope and yelped as a red line of blood oozed from a crack in his rough, raw hand. He wiped the cut on his sleeve. "She rides along, safe inside her cart, doing nothing except giving orders to her Amah and her maidservant. Keep me as far away from her as possible."

"The cart behind hers carries her cook and all their equipment, and I've seen that a boy and girl work there, also," Fourth Brother said. "That cart at the very back is full of gifts for King Galdan. The horse riders never let anyone get near it, but they say it holds the best of the empire's wine and grain, precious gems, silk, and brocades, even books." He looked down the line of soldiers, ten on each side of the carts, barring all access to the princess and her possessions.

"Amah!" the voice from the cart lashed out again. "I am sick of this rain. Make it stop!"

The elderly servant's voice rose in frustration, "Princess Meiling, we are all cold and wet. I cannot control the heavens."

"Then do something to make *me* more comfortable!" the voice demanded.

Chengli glanced again at the horse riders, just as one of them looked down at him and winked. Chengli jerked his head in surprise. What? he thought. Are they sick of listening to her, too? They're worse off than we are. They can't get away! We can! "Come on," he motioned to Fourth Brother, "let's go check the ropes."

They trudged forward along the line of camels and stayed as far from the royal carts as possible. Chengli made a game of trying to count the colorful flags that marked the separate merchants who had joined their group, for the caravan had grown as they traveled. Master Fong alone had a hundred loaded camels, with each set of ten in the care of separate camel drivers. Chengli's set was the last string of ten, and he had them all tied together, head to tail, by ropes looped through their wooden nose pegs, with El Kalid in front. Fourth Brother, with his ten donkeys, followed behind, plus they had extra donkeys and horses to ride, sell for provisions along the way, or use as spares in case of injury. Other travelers had joined them, so that the caravan now included not only merchants with their loaded animals, but also soldiers with their bows and arrows, Buddhist monks in their rough brown robes, and entire families looking for a new life in the hotter, drier lands to the north. All of them trudged along, wet and grumbling in the rain.

As the day wore on, however, the rain slackened and finally stopped. Master chose a resting spot on well-drained land, and the call came down the line to settle for the night. Each group drew together, cooks set up their tents, and all across the soggy field, campfires sent up a friendly glow.

Chengli turned his attention to the animals. He liked keeping them healthy and making them comfortable, but he'd had a hard time learning to deal with the camels. The warmth of early spring made their thick, wooly fur begin to loosen and fall out, but when Chengli first tried to brush it, the camel turned and aimed a mouthful of stinking spit at him. Within the first week, however, he'd learned how to keep the animals calm. Now, one by one, he hobbled the camels so they could not run away during the night, and then he released their packs and examined each one for scratches or sores on its body or thickly padded toes. Next he checked each sack, harness, and rope, and if damaged, he repaired it. Only then, when all his animals had been cared for, could he join the circle in front of the food tent.

He looked around at the men who now shared his life. Tough men, they'd been hardened by endless walking along endless trails. They all wore the same tan hemp tunics and trousers and boots made of pounded wool with the toes and heels reinforced with leather. Chengli's favorite among the workers was the one everyone called Uncle Tao, a grandfatherly man with unruly hair tied in an equally unruly topknot. The hair on his head was black, but his beard was pure white—a curious sight, thought Chengli. Uncle Tao worked as second in command with Master Fong. Together, these two kept their eyes on the entire caravan, checking both men and animals. Uncle Tao often made his way to the end of the line to see that Chengli was learning the finer points of caring for the camels, quietly teaching the boy whatever he needed to understand. From him Chengli learned that their first true rest stop would be at the bustling city of Lanzhou, some five hundred miles northwest of Chang'an. At the slow pace of the heavily loaded camels—twelve or fifteen miles a day—that five hundred miles would take them about eight weeks of walking.

On most nights, when the men gathered for supper, Master Fong and Uncle Tao, as the two highest-ranking men in the group, sat together off to the side, nearly hidden in the shadows, watching, listening, and missing nothing. Chengli sat between the two camel drivers, Bori the Wolf and Abdul, who both came from the far mountains. Abdul was the quiet one, rarely talking but always listening and ready to help. Bori, on the other hand, talked all the time—to people, to the animals, to himself.

It was from Bori that Chengli heard about the three huge waterwheels. "You'll recognize Lanzhou long before we get there," Bori told him, "because you can see the wooden waterwheels, as high as ten stacked camels! They're famous. The buckets lift water out of the Yellow River and dump it into irrigation ditches high up on the cliff. They are so old that nobody knows who built them, but everybody calls them "Mr. Zuo's waterwheels." Chengli thought he must be joking, but it did give him something to watch for.

This night, however, no one talked about the caravan; everyone talked about Princess Meiling.

"Always," Bori said, "that woman is giving orders."

"Orders?" Abdul countered. "She is *ranting* about everything: the road, the cart, the boredom. Why doesn't she get out and walk like the rest of us?"

"What? An imperial princess walking beside camel drivers?" Bori burst into laughter at the ridiculous thought.

"I caught a glimpse of her," Uncle Tao said, "and she is much too old to be sent as a bride. Her hair is gray already. Whatever is our emperor thinking!"

"You're crazy," Abdul shot back. "You must've seen her servant, the Amah. I heard the princess is tall and beautiful."

"Well, just keep her away from me," Bori said as he rolled into his blanket and prepared to sleep. The other men stood, sought out patches of higher ground away from the puddles, wrapped themselves in blankets, and one by one fell asleep.

From the depths of his blanket, Chengli heard Master Fong's voice grumble into the silence. "Where's my jacket? It should be right here in my blanket! This dampness sinks into my old bones. I need my woolen jacket!"

Chengli opened his eyes and wriggled out of his blanket. Next to him, Fourth Brother reached over and shoved him down. "Here, Master," called Fourth Brother. "I'm still awake. I'll help you look. Maybe you hung it on one of the ropes. I'll go look."

"I'll help, too," Chengli said, sitting up again.

"Don't bother. I can do it." Fourth Brother again pushed him down onto his blanket. He lit a torch from the campfire and moved out among the sleeping men and piles of baggage.

Master Fong shook out his blanket again. "That jacket cannot be lost. I wear it every night. The design of scorpions and spiders protects me from the stings and bites of that dreadful desert."

Chengli closed his eyes and against the blackness saw images of huge spiders and snapping scorpions tumbling over each other. He hoped Master Fong's jacket had enough magic to protect the entire caravan. He prayed Fourth Brother would come back with it.

Fourth Brother's voice signaled his return. "Sorry, Master. I poked high and low. I walked on both sides of the line. I found nothing."

Master sank down on his blanket and groaned his displeasure into the blackness of the night.

Morning dawned with a clear blue sky, and the sun shone down on a vast plain of yellow mud. Uncle Tao called out, "Today we enter the walled city of Lanzhou, spread along the banks of the great Yellow River."

"But first," Bori the Wolf called back, "comes this slippery hillside and the narrow Leitan River. Be careful!"

They moved forward along the wide and well-traveled road. With slow, exacting movements, the merchants, beasts, families, and monks picked their way carefully down the slope that tipped the road toward the river. Each silently concentrated on his own safety.

Suddenly, a crash slammed against the hillside.

People screamed.

Camels reared.

Chengli jerked around.

Heading straight for him came a blur of red and gold. The princess's cart careened wildly as it barreled through the mud, shoving in front of it a thrashing, braying donkey caught in the jumbled harness. One wheel cracked and spun out of sight along a rut in the mountainside, causing the cart to tip dangerously as it picked up speed.

Soldiers wheeled their horses around and jumped to the ground to try to stop the cart's downhill skid and free the donkey. Servants tumbled out of the cart, hitting the mud with a sickening splash.

Chengli yelled. Toward him, a small girl-child came catapulting down the rain-filled road, sliding straight into the path of the splintered wheel shaft. Chengli flung himself toward the hurtling child, arms outstretched, grasping for anything to stop her slide.

"The servant girl!" he screamed. "Stop her!"

He slammed into the girl, shoving her away from the broken cart. As he lay sputtering, his body half on top of hers in his attempt to save her, he caught sight of thick black braids encircling her head and sparkling golden jewels threaded among the braids.

"Aiii, it's a *princess*! he bellowed in surprise, dropping her back into the mud.

"Get away from me!" shrieked the princess, as she frantically wiped at her muddy face with her mud-soaked hands. She slapped at Chengli and scrambled to her knees in the mud. "Help *me!*" she screamed to her soldiers. "Forget the stupid cart. Come here and get *me!*"

The princess pushed herself to her feet and stood sobbing, shooing Chengli away and shouting, "How dare you, camel boy? How dare you touch a princess?" She stamped her foot, sending a new layer of mud splashing over her long, silk dress. "Soldiers! Arrest him! Chop off his head!"

The two soldiers who were working to right the fallen cart stopped and slithered through the mud to grab Chengli. He felt his eyes open wide and his heart begin to race. "What was I supposed to do?" he yelled back at the muddy girl-child. "Let you get crushed by the wagon wheel?"

For an answer, a soldier whacked him on the side of the head. "Silence, camel boy! Show respect!"

The princess's Amah, with eyes as round as her chubby face, came slip-sliding toward him, balancing herself against the side of the fallen cart. Behind her came a young, servant boy.

"Come, Princess Meiling," Amah said quietly, reaching for the princess with trembling hands. "We will go wash in the river." She turned to the boy coming up beside her. "Dakshesh, go help repair the cart and tell your sister to come help me with the princess."

Turning back toward the princess, who stood crying and shivering in globs of brown mud, Amah shook her head and looked as if she couldn't decide whether to laugh or cry. "Well, child," she said, "you are a sight. But hush now. Control yourself. That camel boy saved your life."

Amah glanced at the soldiers who still held on to Chengli and gave them a knowing smile. Then holding the princess's arm, she called to the servant girl. "Sudarshana, take her other arm. We will go down to the river."

Once the princess disappeared from sight, Chengli pulled himself away from the soldiers' loosened grip and ran sliding down the hill to where the rest of the men worked at calming the terrified animals. He threw himself into the midst of the group of workers.

"Did you see *that*?" he gasped. "Did you *see* that? The princess—she's a child. She's littler than me!"

four

Chengli dragged himself away from the crowd of workers, found his camel, and shoved himself up tight against El Kalid's rough side, willing himself invisible. His thoughts circled: I'm a dead man—I meant to help—I thought she was a servant—I never meant to touch the princess.

He looked downhill. The princess was out of sight. He looked uphill. The soldiers were all bent over their work on the broken cart. He left the safety of El Kalid's side and worked his way downhill until he came to Master Fong.

"Illustrious Master, I am truly a useless camel boy," he said, looking up into Master Fong's face, gruff and dark. Quickly, he looked back down at the ground. "Please, Master, hide me! The princess has ordered my head chopped off! You said we would rest this week, here in the Lanzhou caravanserai. Let me stay in the courtyard and guard the loads. I'll stay inside the walls all week. I'll never, never go near the princess again!"

The caravansary, like every other caravan inn along the route, offered protection from wild animals and thieving humans. Four walls surrounded an inner courtyard where packs and animals could be stored with safety, and along each side, built into the walls, were open alcoves offering shelter to the men. Large cities often had ten or even one hundred inns on their outskirts. Here in Lanzhou, the men said there were fifty, and the merchants divided their caravans among them. The princess, Chengli knew, would have her very own inn, keeping her away from the smells and dirt of the men, packs, and animals.

"Get up!" Master Fong ordered. "Yes, you may hide all week, if that's what you wish. There is always work to be done inside the caravansary. But put away your fear; she cannot order the loss of your head. She may think she has that power, but at her age it is only in thought, not reality. You are quite safe." The master turned away but swung back to face Chengli. "Speaking of your head . . . why is your hair falling free and messy? Why is it not tied in a proper knot at the back of your head?"

Chengli mumbled an answer.

"Speak up, boy!" thundered Master Fong. "When I ask, you answer!"

Chengli winced and spoke as fast as he could. "I got nits in my hair and Old Cook cut it all off."

Master reached out and yanked at the strands of Chengli's black, unruly hair. "It's long now," he laughed. "Go get a strip of cloth and tie it up properly!"

Chengli grabbed the nearest rag and tied up his hair in an untidy version of the common topknot. He then sat down to consider the caravansary. He looked up at the high stone walls of the inn's courtyard and found that just looking at them made him feel safe and far removed from the princess. He walked over to Abdul and Bori and began to unload the packs. Abdul pointed to Chengli's tightly knotted hair and grinned his approval.

During the week, the men divided the work. Some cared for the animals outside the walls of Lanzhou. Some protected the loads stacked inside the many caravansaries scattered across the city. Others took off time to explore the huge city and visit the bazaar, buying supplies, eating fresh fruit, and laughing at the acrobats who performed on many street corners.

One day midweek, Fourth Brother appeared in the gateway. "Ho, Skinny One! Are you in there?" he yelled. "I've got news and food. Which do you want first?"

Chengli poked his head out of his small alcove. "Come on in—and start with the food."

"I've been to the bazaar, and I got this savory flatbread covered with onions and garlic." He held out the huge disk of hard bread for Chengli to get a whiff of the aroma. Chengli grabbed the flat disk, tore off a part, and munched happily.

"And," Fourth Brother continued, "I have news about the princess."

Chengli choked and spit the bread across the yard. "I don't want to hear anything about her!" He brushed a fly off the loaf, as if wiping the princess out of his life.

"Yes, you do. I saw her two young servants, those two from India. They were also at the bazaar, and Sudarshana said to tell you that the princess seems to be her regular self again. She's still grumbling, but now it's because she is bored. She is tired of the cramped courtyard where she has been kept for safety. She misses the road. Can you believe it?" He laughed and punched at Chengli. "Even traveling with us is better than sitting still!"

Chengli groaned and put his head down on his knees. He forgot about the flat bread in his lap, and onion and garlic smeared all across his face. "What should I do?"

"If you ask me, just pretend nothing ever happened."

"Easy for you to say," Chengli said, wiping his face with his sleeve. "No one ordered your head chopped off!"

At the end of the week, word came to load up and move on. The long string of camels complained with grunts and groans as their handlers shouted and prodded them into action. They headed out of the city to the northwest, gawked at Mr. Zuo's famous waterwheels, and moved into the corridor where the land slowly changed. On their left loomed mountains so high that the snow never melted—a place called Tibet was up there somewhere, Bori said. On the right, farmers' fields gave way to hot, dry plains and finally to gray-brown stone. In this harsh land, rivers shriveled to creeks. Creeks dried into puddles. Then even the puddles disappeared.

Chengli grinned. It felt good to be on the move again. The sun beamed dry and warm, the loads stayed in place, and even the animals seemed to walk with a bounce in their step. Chengli took off the woolen blanket he wore wrapped around his shoulders for warmth and threw it up over the pack on El Kalid's back.

The princess grumbled less, but Fourth Brother grumbled more. Chengli watched him slap at the donkeys.

"What's going on? You're usually the happy one," Chengli called out.

"I asked Master when I could work with the guards. We are going out into wild territory now. We need more guards. All he said was that I could be one of the night crew. Night crew? Staying awake all night and banging on pots and pans just to let night raiders know I'm awake and watching?" Fourth Brother slapped at the donkey. "Pots and pans! Ha! In Chang'an Master said that I could learn to use the bow and arrows, and maybe even the whip chain." His eyes narrowed and he kicked at the stones underfoot. "He promised!" Fourth Brother continued to sulk along, now in silence.

Chengli walked along and watched his friend. His anger is different from mine, Chengli thought. I yell and holler and then I'm over it. Fourth Brother holds his anger in and just complains as it grows. What will he do when he can't hold it in any longer? With no answer, Chengli turned his attention back to the camels.

The days marched along one after the other, and although it was still spring, it felt more and more like summer. Chengli liked best the days when they passed the mud-walled, high-gated garrison towns like Wuwei and Zhangye, both busy with soldiers inside and out, protecting the emperor's territory. Along this corridor, hemmed in by mountains on one side and desert on the other, the soldiers raised thousands of horses for the emperor. Sometimes Chengli saw the horses galloping free in the distance. Other times he saw soldiers practicing with bows and arrows, crossbows, or even fire arrows.

One of the fire-arrow-shooting soldiers called out a warning. "Take care!" he said. "The road grows more dangerous. Set your guards out both day and night."

"So are you worried, Skinny One?"

Chengli looked up to see four Buddhist monks ambling along together, slowly letting the caravan pass them by until they had dropped behind to walk with him.

"We heard about your excitement with the princess last week," the youngest monk said. "Quite a story."

Fourth Brother tied the rope of his lead donkey to the back of Chengli's end camel and sauntered up to join the monks. "How far are you going?" he asked them. "Your packs are awfully small." He pointed to the blanket rolls that each monk carried on his back.

"We go to the end of the Great Wall, to the town of Dunhuang."

"Dunhuang?" Fourth Brother asked. "That's a check-point where they inspect loads and collect taxes. But you have no load."

"We are headed to a wondrous place outside the town," the young monk answered. "There is a steep ravine cut by an ancient river where a whole row of temples honoring Buddha has been hollowed out of the face of the cliff. We are going there to work on a new cave temple."

"We'll paint the walls," the old monk said. "We've planned a picture to show what life is like today—the houses, the fields, even the caravans. I'll paint you, your camels, your donkeys," he said to Fourth Brother. "Even your brown hat will be in my painting."

"I plan to paint another wall with a picture of the Buddha and then surround him with pictures of all the stories he told," said a chubby monk. "That way, people who cannot read will see and understand."

Suddenly Dakshesh's voice, with its lilting Indian accent, broke into their quiet conversation. "Our princess gives an order!" called Dakshesh as he ran forward to join them, his short, brown tunic flapping against his legs. "Princess has been watching from behind the window of her cart. She has never seen all of you talking together like this, and she wants to know what you talk about."

"Princess Meiling," Sudarshana added, running up to join her brother, "orders us to take her your news." The servant girl fell into step beside Chengli.

"Well, there is a bit of news," the young monk said, "but we haven't even mentioned it yet. If we keep going at this pace, we should arrive in the city of Dunhuang around the fifth day of the fifth month. Every year on that day, the king of the city invites the people out to Crescent Lake, a spot where the gravel desert disappears into the great sand dunes of the Taklamakan Desert. There the king provides all the people an entire day of feasting, games, and climbing on the huge sand mountains."

"There can't be a lake in the sand dunes!" exclaimed Sudarshana.

"Ah, but wait until you see it," said the young monk. "Perhaps it is magic, for the dunes are huge, and they rise all around the little lake, yet they never cover it. It has been that way since time began."

"But I'm afraid of the sand," said Chengli. "People say the sand goes on and on, and it all looks the same, and people get lost and die there."

"Not the dunes by Crescent Lake," replied the monk, "and that is why the king holds the festival there. People do not cross over the dunes into the endless desert but climb instead to the top of the nearest ones and then slide down. They climb up for the joy of sliding down, just as people who live in the snow feel joy when sliding down their snow-covered hills."

"None of us have ever lived in the snow," said Dakshesh. "We've never slid anywhere except in rain puddles."

"And in mud," grumbled Chengli, reluctantly remembering his run-in with the princess.

"People attend the festival to become like children again, sliding down the huge sand mountains and watching the acrobats, dancers, and musicians. People talk about it all year!" the monk continued.

"Ho! What fun that would be—to play instead of work!" Chengli threw his wide straw hat into the air, reached out and grabbed Dakshesh's belt, pulling him around in a wild circle and yelling at the top of his lungs.

"What are you doing?" laughed Fourth Brother as he tripped over his own feet to join the chase. "We don't live in Dunhuang, so the party's not for us."

The monks joined arms and circled around Dakshesh. "Well, those who do go can all pretend to be children again for that one day. That's the fun of it."

A shrill call cut through the laughter. "Come here to me this minute!"

The voice of the princess froze their actions and ended their playfulness. Dakshesh and Sudarshana turned and scurried around the royal soldiers to walk beside the cart and tell the princess this latest news. Fourth Brother dashed back to his donkeys, and Chengli turned toward his camels.

"Skinny One!" the princess's voice filled the silence. "You, the skinny one, do not turn away. Come here to me."

Chengli looked at Fourth Brother in desperation. "Help me," he whispered. "I can't go there."

"Attend my cart!" called the princess to Chengli.

Chengli looked at the monks. They turned away. He looked at the soldiers. They turned away. He grabbed at his hat, pulled it down so tight it scratched his forehead, and walked back to stand beside the royal cart. I've got to be careful, he thought. She's young, but she rules over me. She is royalty; I am nobody. He stared at the ground, hoping to show respect.

"Camel boy, you must do as I ask. You are in no position to disobey my wishes," came the voice from behind the silk curtain. "I heard what the monks said, and I want to go to the party. I want to play on the sand dunes."

"Princess, I work for Master Fong. I cannot play. I must care for his animals," Chengli replied.

"He can do without you for one day," the princess stated shrilly.

"Princess, truly, I cannot help you," Chengli repeated. He stared at the ground and tried to think, but all he could come up with was: Master Fong will fire me. The princess will hate me. The monks cannot help me.

He looked at Sudarshana. She looked at the ground. He scrunched his eyes shut and forced his thoughts to calm.

"You," the voice became harsh with power, "you *will* get me invited to the celebration."

"But . . ."

"Do it."

"I can't," Chengli groaned, "I am nobody."

"Ask!"

The silk curtain closed.

five

CHENGLI WASN'T HUNGRY. He hunched down in the dinner circle and stared. At nothing. He sat without eating, listening to the voice that pushed and pulled his mind the same way his spirit wind used to push and shove his body. His head rang with the voice from the cart, over and over, again and again. Ask, it said, I give you no choice.

In about a week, they should reach Dunhuang, and Chengli had no idea what he should do. He stood up, determined to ask Master Fong for guidance.

"Out of my way!" bellowed the master. Master Fong strode into the camp circle and shoved Chengli aside without even noticing who he was.

"Where is the thief? I will rip him apart!" The scar on Master Fong's cheek quivered with rage. "My elegant inkstone . . . an inkstone worthy of the emperor's treasures! With it I must fill out all the required travel declarations to give to the inspectors when we reach Dunhuang. Without the documents, we will not be allowed out through the gate. And without the inkstone, there will be no documents! It is gone! Only a gremlin could know where I kept it. It could

not have simply fallen out on the road." He glared at each
of his men. "Don't just sit there!" he roared, his whole body
trembling. "Find it!"

The men dropped their supper bowls, spilling the spicy
noodles and cabbage in all directions. They leaped to their
feet and scattered. Chengli ran from the circle, dashing this
way and that way, searching the ground until he bumped
into Fourth Brother slowly making his way back to the
campfire.

"Master is so careless," said Fourth Brother. "First he
loses his jacket and now this!"

"Come on, we can find it for him," said Chengli.

"Relax! It must be gone, for I've looked all around and
couldn't find it. Things lost in this desert disappear forever!"
Fourth Brother shrugged and went to eat his meal.

Sure enough, each man returned from the search empty
handed. They sat in silence trying to ignore the scowl on the
face of their master, and in silence they finished their meal.

Morning came, and with it their lives took on the
predictable rhythm. The caravan moved northward with
the slow speed of heavily laden camels. Day after day they
trudged along between the mountains on the left and the gray,
gravelly desert on the right. Herds of wild camels peppered
the horizon. Mounds of sand lay trapped, tight against tufts
of brown desert scrub bushes, dried out and prickly.

Chengli had stared in amazement the day they passed
the end of the Great Wall. Somehow, he'd thought the wall
just kept going. And there it was . . . the end. It made him
a little uneasy to realize he was actually leaving the Middle
Kingdom, the China he had always known. Now China was

behind him, and ahead were the deserts he'd heard of only in stories. To his right, as far as he could see, stretched the gray stones of the Gobi> To his left, just coming into view, lay the boundless sweep of the Taklamakan sand, drier, and hotter, he'd been told, than any place known to man.

Chengli used to brag to Little Limp that he knew all about caravans, but bit by bit now he realized he hardly knew anything at all. He hadn't known where China ended. He didn't know about the cities outside of China along the edge of the desert. Oasis cities, Bori called them, because each one could only exist right at the base of a mountain where a river came down from the melting snow. When the river disappeared under the sand of the desert, the city and the farms around it just stopped. Nothing could live without that water.

And kings! Oh, the kings that Bori talked about. Each one of those desert cities had its own ruler. Imagine! A different king each time the caravan stopped. Chengli got confused just thinking about it. Abdul said the kings were like little emperors, each one ruling his own city. It had to be that way, he thought, because each city stood alone, with hundreds and hundreds of miles of desert between it and the next oasis. So, for something to do during the boredom of walking, Chengli memorized the names of each city—Dunhuang, Hami, Turpan, Kucha, and finally, Kashgar—and wondered what he'd find in each of them. Would anyone know about his father?

As they got closer to Dunhuang, Chengli thought again of the princess's demand and wondered how to fulfill it, but no answer came. Then one night, he awoke. He watched the moon slide slowly across the sky, and with it his mind slid across his ideas and discarded them into the night. Discarded all but one, that is, and the more he thought on it, the better it sounded. Finally he rolled out of his blanket, crept across the dark, shadowed ground to Fourth Brother, and shook him awake.

"Fourth Brother, I have an idea, but I'll need your help."

"For this you wake me in the middle of the night? Wait till morning," grumbled the older boy.

"No. Listen to me," Chengli pleaded.

"Not now."

"Yes, now! I need you."

"Hey, boy! Go away! Let me sleep."

"No."

"Fine! I'm awake now. What do you want?" Fourth Brother sat up and hugged his blanket around his shoulders.

"I know how we can get the princess to the party, but I need your help." Chengli pulled himself closer to Fourth Brother and lowered his voice. "Once we get to Dunhuang, the monks told me they will leave our caravan and join the family of the king who rules Dunhuang. That family is going to the cave temple to have their portrait painted on one of the walls there!"

"What's that got to do with our princess?" Fourth Brother mumbled.

"That's what I'm telling you. Just stay awake! For us to get the permission our princess demands for the fifth-day celebration, we just have to follow the monks. They said they planned to join up with the royal family. So we follow them, go up to the most important-looking man who surely will be the king, introduce ourselves, and tell him about our princess."

"You're dumber than a rock! Kings are rich and wear silk and gold and rubies, and they don't listen to dirty, smelly caravan workers." He grabbed his blanket and pulled it tight over his head to shield his neck from the chill of the night.

"Do you have a better idea?"

"I have no idea at all. I don't need any ideas. The princess gave the order to *you*, not to me," Fourth Brother said.

Chengli yanked the blanket away from his friend's face and kept whispering, "I know I am a tiger by birth, and that should make me strong enough. But," he hesitated, "I also know that you have never lacked for ideas. By myself, I'd never think of the right thing to say." Chengli gently poked the older boy. "You always know the best words to use!"

"Emmm," Fourth Brother paused, then chuckled. "You're right about that. It's worth a try." He rolled back down into his blanket and covered his head. "Now go to sleep!" came the muffled order.

Trudging northward, the caravan left the protection of the mountains and started around the edge of the great sand desert. Chengli thought about the city of Dunhuang and wondered what they would trade there. He knew that ninety of master's camels were loaded with treasures to be sold at the far end of their route, but the last ten camels—his camels—had items they could trade at the oasis towns along the way, giving them fresh food and more water for their journey.

Thus every day his curiosity grew, until Dunhuang seemed a magical place. Full of such thoughts, he loaded and unloaded the camels, gathered more sweat and dirt on his clothing and more calluses on his feet. Finally the cry echoed along the line, "Oasis! Dunhuang!"

And sure enough, far off in the distance, above the green of the oasis, Chengli could just make out the massive, red-brick tower with its two arching roofs that signaled the gate to the city. As they moved nearer, they came to the farmers' huts, lush orchards, and colorful gardens, all watered by channels of water brought from the river—a real river! The road followed the canal, and Chengli grinned from ear to ear as he walked past travelers resting along the water's edge or lighting sticks of incense to place on an altar of the river dragon.

This city of Dunhuang ranked as an official checkpoint for people entering or leaving China. Inspectors gave the stamp of approval to legal traders and checked for smugglers who tried to get illegal items in or out of China. As such, it bustled with activity. Noise and confusion bubbled in all directions. Caravans reported their wares with all the details of where it came from, where it was going, plus the size and weight of each camel's load. Soldiers patrolled. Inspectors inspected. Tax collectors collected import and export taxes. Caravans moved through passport and animal control as they entered and left the safety of the Middle Kingdom.

Chengli knew they would take one of his camels and empty its load at the market, selling iron tools to the men and bronze mirrors and colorful pottery to the women, along with the bricks of hard, packed tea and bags of rice. This city had nearly as many people as Chang'an, and they all wanted the same luxuries as people farther south and were willing to pay for them. In exchange, the caravan could get the dried food it needed: noodles, fish, figs, persimmons, and vegetables to keep the group going to the next town.

On the day when Master Fong and Uncle Tao met with the customs officials, Chengli saw the monks gather their belongings and stride off toward the city. He called to Fourth Brother, and both boys ran to fall in step behind the monks.

"Go back," the young monk cautioned.

"No. We must follow you," Chengli answered, and they trailed behind the monks as they walked toward the gateway with its watchtower topped by double roofs of clay tiles and, Chengli noticed, a guardian dragon perched high above on the ridge line.

They reached the cool shadow of the city wall just as the royal procession came out through the archway of the gate, flanked by soldiers standing at attention and a row of red lanterns hung for the festive occasion. The king's wooden carriage was small, but it had a broad umbrella protecting the riders from the scorching sun and four horses covered with golden bells and bright red tassels pulling it slowly forward. Servants in blue gowns followed behind on foot. Everyone carried gifts to leave at the temple for the monks who were painting the wall murals of the Buddha. These devoted men asked for no pay for their work and lived only on the gifts people gave to them. It was the way folks thanked them for the beautiful paintings they put on the temple walls.

Chengli stared as the procession passed by, and his legs suddenly lost their will to move. This is not going to work, he thought. No one will listen to us. No one will even notice us.

"Aiii!" A blur of orange flashed in front of Chengli's eyes. He crumpled to the ground in fear, clamping his arms over the top of his head.

Feeling nothing, he forced his eyes open. Flaming arrows stuck out of the gravel in front of him, blocking his path. He glanced sideways. Fourth Brother also crouched with his face squashed into the ground. Boots appeared right in front of his nose. Chengli looked up. Soldiers stood in front of him with knives at their waists and bows drawn.

"What is this?" the first soldier barked. "Sand urchins dare approach the royal family?"

Chengli's stomach lurched, and words banged around in his head like warriors in combat: failure . . . prison . . . hard labor. Master Fong would fire him. Or sell him as a slave!

Fourth Brother's voice cut through Chengli's whirling thoughts. "Live forever, strong protector! We are your servants. We are simple desert boys, but we bring a message from our own noble princess."

Chengli stopped shaking and his mind cleared. How could Fourth Brother talk like that—like he wasn't afraid of anything?

"Your ruler's nobility, his splendor, is known to all," Fourth Brother continued.

I never heard of their ruler before, thought Chengli.

"If he wishes these humble ones to approach, we shall do so," Fourth Brother stated simply, as secure with his words as a royal ambassador.

The soldier chuckled. "Stand up, fast-talking urchin!" he ordered. "And spit the sand out of your mouth." He waited while Fourth Brother did as he was told. "Now, who is this princess? And why does she have desert scum do her errands?"

Fourth Brother explained about their caravan, the princess they were escorting, and her wish to attend the famous party at the sand dunes. While he talked, the fire arrows burned themselves out, and the soldier put his arrow back in the quiver.

Chengli had a new thought. Perhaps he, too, could play at this game of wits. He stood and cleared his throat.

"My shadow is small before the blazing sun of your strength," he said to the soldier. "But this small boy was sent on the errand because he accidentally insulted Princess Meiling, who comes from the emperor's court in Chang'an, and she has chosen this quest as his penance. We desire to ask for a safe conduct document to allow our imperial princess to attend the party at Singing Sand Dunes. She is a very young princess and would like to have one day to behave as a child."

"Stay here," the soldier ordered. He strode away, muttering "emperor" and "Chang'an." He soon returned with a wooden ticket printed with the red seal of the magistrate's family. "Carry this to your princess. Tell her Dunhuang welcomes her."

六
six

ON THE FIFTH DAY OF THE FIFTH MONTH, Princess Meiling perched tall and straight on a clean blanket draped over El Kalid's wooden saddle. Amah had made certain that the princess honor her emperor by dressing in her most royal clothing. Her pale blue tunic and baggy trousers were covered by a long robe of green-and-gold silk with wide sleeves edged in a pattern of blue flowers, and on top of that came a short red-and-gold silk apron. A string of green jade and red rubies wound in and out of her hair, braided and piled high on top of her head—all calling attention to her status as princess from the family of the Chinese emperor.

"She looks beautiful," said Chengli.

"She doesn't look like a child now," Fourth Brother answered. "She's a true princess!"

Chengli's success in getting the safe conduct ticket had startled Master Fong so much that he forgot to be angry with the boys for leaving their work. He even lent the camel El Kalid to the princess and two donkeys to her servants for them to ride to the dunes in style. Princess Meiling, neglecting to thank Master Fong, ordered Fourth Brother and Chengli to tend the animals. Master Fong did not argue.

Meiling's attendants scrambled to find their proper place to begin this unusual day. Chengli stood aside and watched as Amah gave the orders. First came the princess. On each side of the newly royal camel rode two of her personal guards, with daggers shining at their waists and bows and arrows on their backs. Following behind walked Fourth Brother, leading the donkeys that carried the young servants, Dakshesh and Sudarshana. Amah, saying she was much too old for such things, chose to stay with the caravan. She waved Chengli to the front of the line.

"Me? To the front?" With a jolt, Chengli realized that he was going along. When he had gotten permission for the princess, he had never imagined that he would be allowed to go with her.

Amah again waved him forward. He grabbed El Kalid's rope and strutted out in front of the group, doing a little dance as he slid under the loop of rope to the other side of the camel. He grinned up at the princess—he couldn't help it. He didn't even mind being her servant for a day, because what a day this promised to be!

The cool morning air and the promise of food and fun set everyone, even the royal soldiers, to humming and singing tunelessly. As they reached the gathering place by the Crescent Lake, the sand dunes rose up like mountains in front of them, and the road disappeared from view under the dust of hundreds of donkey carts overflowing with families headed for the celebration.

The soldiers guided their small group to the sparkling blue lake and tethered the animals so they could get water and tethered them to the ropes provided. Already kites flew in the sky, acrobats and jugglers warmed up their acts, and under a huge canopy, servants stocked banquet tables with bronze dishes, wooden platters, ceramic bowls, chopsticks, and the promise of elegant, savory foods.

Princess Meiling stood primly, unsure where to turn or what to do. Dakshesh, Sudarshana, and Fourth Brother looked around eagerly but also remained still, waiting until the princess gave orders. Chengli pointed to the distant spots of color that moved up and down on the sand dunes—people struggling up and then sliding down gleefully on the soft, silky sand.

A grandmother walked by, her grandson tied snuggly on her back. She noticed the children's confusion and joined them, bowing slightly to the princess. "You may climb up the dunes from wherever you like," she said. "There is no set route. And you needn't be afraid of being injured, for the sand is very soft. Watch and see. Some people go barefoot, others sit or even crawl on the hills. I think, once you get used to it, you will never want to leave."

Thanking the grandmother and clearly gathering her courage, Meiling led her four attendants across the hard-packed sand to the base of the dunes, followed by two of her soldiers, who stood at the base of the dunes to keep a careful watch.

"I don't like the sound," Meiling said, stopping and squinting her eyes. "The sand roars like thunder."

"It's the demons," Fourth Brother backed away. "I'm not going up there!"

"Wait!" called Chengli. "You just think you hear demons. It's the sand moving. Look, when people climb on it, it makes the sand slip and roll, and that's what makes it roar. That's why they call it Singing Sand. Come on, let's go!"

Fourth Brother still looked worried, but he came back and stood beside Chengli and waited until Meiling started up the hill of sand.

"Help! Help me! I'm slipping!" Suddenly giggling, Meiling tried again. Up a step, slide back a step. The soft sand, tender and fine, flowed into each footprint like water flowing into a cup. Up a step, slide back with the pouring sand. Meiling dragged herself slowly upward, gasping for breath and laughing in between the gasps.

"Go faster, and you won't slide back!" called Dakshesh, forgetting to keep a respectful distance and leaping up through the sand to join her. Chengli and Fourth Brother stumbled onto all fours and dug at the sand as they followed Dakshesh up to the ridge.

"I can't do it! My clothes are just too heavy!" Meiling stopped climbing and unfastened the cord that held her red-and-gold apron.

Sudarshana grabbed at the apron. "Mistress, you can't take off your royal clothes! Not here."

"I can, and I will!" Off came the red apron and tiny, red slippers. Sudarshana's face turned pale with fright, but having no choice, she picked up the clothing, folded it neatly, and set it in a pile to mark their path up the dune.

Up they went, faster now, until Meiling stopped again.

She looked up. Her voice carried plainly along the wall of sand. "Boys wear only their tunic and baggy pants. That's why they climb so fast," she said.

"Princess, no!" Sudarshana pleaded.

"Yes," snapped Meiling. "Have you never heard of the girl Fu Hao? She lived long ago, and she rode horses and led an army. She didn't have to wear heavy, silk gowns." Off came the silk brocade gown.

Sudarshana picked it up and set it down in the sand. Then she looked down at her own heavy clothes and laughed. Off came her blue-striped outer tunic, which she folded and set beside the clothing of the princess. Soon Meiling and her servant, giggling like sisters, reached the high ridge clad only in their blue trousers and tunics.

"Here's an order," Meiling frowned as she looked down at the piles that marked their progress up the dune. "Don't you, any of you, ever *ever* tell Amah, or I'll . . ."

Chengli winced, but Fourth Brother laughed. "We know," he said, "you'll chop off our heads!"

Meiling stiffened at the reference, and her eyes flashed with anger. Just as quickly, she relaxed and giggled. "Just don't tell my Amah," she repeated.

Cut off from real life below, the children felt the morning slip quickly by. When Chengli turned to look over his shoulder, he saw just what the monks had told him he would . . . nothing, absolutely nothing but an endless flow of sand mountains rising and falling, reaching farther than he could see, going on forever across thousands of miles.

This was the sand desert where people died; this was the desert the villagers called "go in and you won't come

out" desert. He shuddered, turned back, and looked down
at the festival around Crescent Lake.

Chengli longed to go down and join the excitement,
but no one could go down until the princess was ready. So
instead, he sat on the ridge of sand and watched people at
the base of the dune coming and going. He even cheered
for a passionate tug-of-war fanned by beating drums and
yelling crowds.

Sitting there high above the crowd, their ranks as highest
and lowest—princess and servants—gradually faded, and
they began sharing their true thoughts. It started when
Dakshesh became brave enough to ask why the people
called their country the Middle Kingdom.

"It's a funny name," he said. "It's the middle of what?"

Meiling said the ancient people didn't know about other
countries and thought they were living in the middle of the
civilized world. "So ever since then," she said, "Chinese people
use the symbols for "middle" and "country" to mean China."

"Old Cook told me," Chengli chimed in, "that people in
Chang'an say it's in the middle because a person can walk
ten days in any direction and still be in China!"

"Ha!" Dakshesh hit the sand and sent a shower into the
air, "Whoever said that didn't live out *here*. We've already
walked out of China!"

Meiling, laughing, sent a spray of sand back at him, but
the question set each one thinking.

Sitting beside Sudarshana, Meiling stared into the
distance, and her face became wistful. "Sometimes I
wonder how it feels—being in a family. Look at all the
donkey carts down there. They are like tiny toys on a rug

of sand, with children climbing in and jumping out." She stood and brushed sand off her lap. "Donkey carts are so dirty! A princess must never be dirty." She sat down again, pouting at some unspoken thought.

"It didn't help me, being in a family," Fourth Brother said. "Four boys made one too many for my father. He gave me to Master Fong. The caravan is my family."

Meiling stretched out on the warm sand, picked up handfuls, and let it sift slowly through her fingers. "I never saw my father, really. He is a cousin to the emperor, but you know, the emperor has many relatives, and each has many children. My father never had time for his children, especially his daughters."

Chengli listened and thought about his own father. He didn't feel like talking, so he poked in the sand instead.

"What about the families of the caravan men?" Meiling asked. "Some of those men are fathers, and they leave their homes for years at a time!"

"Are all fathers so busy they forget their children?" Dakshesh asked. "Our father brought us from India to bring gifts to the emperor."

"And when he had to return suddenly," Sudarshana picked up the story, "he just left us. 'Serve the princess,' he said. 'You'll have a good life.' I wish we could find a caravan headed for India. I'd rather go home."

Anger flashed across Meiling's face. "I'm *good* to you. You should be happy to . . ." She stopped and looked slowly from Sudarshana to Dakshesh. "Oh . . . I never thought . . . you long for your real home just the way I long to go back to Chang'an!"

Chengli listened to all this talk of family, rolled over onto his stomach, and stretched across the crest of the dune. He cushioned his cheek in the sand. He blinked sand out of his eyes. He coughed sand from his throat. He fingered the pouch attached to his belt and kept silent. A broken piece of jade, he thought. That's all I have of my father—not even a memory. The soldiers had tried to help him that first day they arrived in Dunhuang. They'd asked around the garrison and had come back to tell him that some old men recognized the name of Inspector Chao Changwon, but that's all. No one had heard of him in years, they'd said. Not in years. They didn't even remember what he looked like.

The princess laughed a coughing sort of laugh, and Chengli's thoughts scattered.

"Well, it doesn't help to mope," Meiling said. "It's strange how we've changed up here. We sound like friends, talking this way." She paused and looked out across the dunes. "I've never had friends." She looked from Dakshesh to Sudarshana to Chengli to Fourth Brother, then stood up and smoothed the glistening silk of her royal bloomers. "I am a princess. I have servants, and," she added, "I now order us all to go down and be part of the celebration! Everybody up!"

"Hooray!"

"Let's go!"

They slid, rolled, and leaped down the long slope, picking up speed as they went. The walking turned to running, and the running turned to flying with arms like windmills and legs thrashing. Laughing, they reached the bottom with sand in their hair, sand in their clothes, and sand flying out from between their toes.

"The old grandmother was right! I don't want to stop," cried Dakshesh. "Let's go up again."

So they climbed back up and slid down once, twice, three times until finally exhausted, the princess announced her hunger. The girls stopped to gather up their cast-off clothes, shake the sand out of them, and dress to make themselves presentable again. The soldiers on guard stretched and grinned, happy to finally get to move on into the crowd. Then the group spent the rest of the afternoon going from stall to stall sampling the rice cakes, bean cakes, and sticky rice candy. They watched the acrobats, cheered wildly at the games of tug-of-war, lingered along the row of stalls selling ribbons, tops, hats, dolls, even cricket cages, and then finally returned to the tables to taste delicious morsels of dried, salted squid and baby octopus.

As the sun slid down the sky to touch the top of the sand mountains, Meiling looked at each companion and shook her head. When she spoke, she was princess once again. "Fourth Brother and Skinny One, go tell the royal soldiers that we are ready to return."

Chengli followed Fourth Brother to the small lake, where people continued to enjoy the leftover food still spread beneath the colorful canopy.

Fourth Brother called out, "Skinny One, go ahead without me. I'll be there in a minute." He swerved through the crowd of well-dressed families and pushed past them into the cluster of animal tenders.

Curious, Chengli followed. Fourth Brother began gesturing excitedly as a crowd gathered round him. Chengli watched him hold out a small box and open it. The crowd sucked in an appreciative breath.

Chengli pushed in closer to get a better look. "Aiii, you can't sell that!" He elbowed his way through the crowd and grabbed at Fourth Brother. In the same breath, the men standing around him yelled, "Thief! Thief!" and yanked him away.

"No!" Chengli called out as he struggled to get out of their grasp. "Not me! Him! That's Master Fong's inkstone."

The men shoved Chengli back to the ground and stepped over him to get a better look at Fourth Brother's treasure. "Get away, boy," ordered one of the men.

"But he stole it. He—"

"Shut your mouth!" Fourth Brother muttered, his voice hard and mean. "I found it in the sand. Not in his bedroll. Not on his donkey. In the *sand*. It could be anybody's, and now it's *mine*." Ignoring Chengli, he bartered skillfully, the box quickly sold, and the men drifted away. The money went into Fourth Brother's pouch.

"There, now you've seen it. I told you I'd get back at the master for breaking his promise to me."

"But you're a thief!" Chengli protested.

"What's it to you?"

"You've been stealing all along!"

"Never from a friend. Never from you." Fourth Brother grinned, then his voice softened. "You should join me." He opened his arms in a welcoming gesture.

Chengli pulled back, startled.

"No, really! I can teach you," said Fourth Brother. "You'll never get caught. You'll make more money than your tiny caravan wage, I promise you that. You could be a professional, you look so innocent!"

"I don't think so." Chengli thought of his poor wages and wavered. "It would be great to have good food to eat and money to buy things at the bazaar, but . . ." He thought of the father he had never known. "My father was an *inspector*. He was honest—Old Cook said so—and I am his son!" He turned away, his hand fingering the jade tied to his belt. "I will honor his spirit!"

"No one will know."

"I . . ."

Fourth Brother laughed and placed his arm around Chengli's shoulder. "You tell anybody what you just saw, and you won't have to worry about your father's spirit. I will haunt you myself for the rest of your life." He grinned innocently, moving his hands like a snake charmer's in front of Chengli, making the younger boy think of two floating ghost tendrils. "Join me—join me," he chanted.

"I . . . I . . . I will *not*."

"All right, have it your way. But you tell anybody about me, and I'll wring your scrawny neck!" The smile slid from Fourth Brother's face.

Chengli stood still as reality sank in. "You took Master Fong's jacket, didn't you? The scorpion jacket. The one that protects him on the desert. You're nothing but a smuggler! You . . . you son of scorpions!"

Fourth Brother stepped in front of Chengli, his ghost tendril hands turned into clenched fists. His eyes narrowed and glistened like a snake about to strike. "Tell and you're dead, o innocent one."

He turned away abruptly and walked off into the crowd.

seven

THE NEXT INSTANT, Chengli found himself standing alone in a swirl of anger as Fourth Brother swaggered away to collect the two donkeys. Here he'd caught Fourth Brother with stolen goods, stolen from the very man who had helped him and given him a job. Yet, Chengli thought, I don't dare say a word! He tried to breathe slowly. He talked to his spirit father. He thought of Old Cook. Useless. All useless. He remained furious at Fourth Brother but realized there was nothing he could do.

Scowling, he watched the older boy present the donkeys to Dakshesh and Sudarshana with a flourish. "Here, my royal friends, are your mighty steeds." With a grin, he reached out and helped first Dakshesh and then Sudarshana mount their donkeys.

Chengli nodded to the group. "I'll be with you in a minute," he called and turned away. He walked in a long, slow circle, shoving at stones with his foot and shoving at thoughts in his mind. I must calm my anger before I go back to the princess, he thought.

He knew it was Fourth Brother's fast talking that had allowed them to have this special day. But with the same ease, Fourth Brother's words had also disposed of stolen property. Anger now stood between them. Fourth Brother rattled off any words at all to get whatever he wanted from people. Chengli knew that, had known it all along, but today those words had yanked him up to the best experience and down to the very worst.

He kicked another stone and pounded the air with his fists, violently at first, and then softer and softer, forcing his temper under control.

"Let's go!" Dakshesh called.

"I'm coming," Chengli answered.

Everyone seemed to feel the change of mood as they started off with heavy, labored plodding. The horses, the donkeys, even El Kalid, put their feet down in slow dragging rhythm. Even the imperial guards ambled slowly along beside them. Tired, thought Chengli, we are all so tired. He surely was exhausted by the day of fantasy and friendship and then the crash back into the depths of reality. His goal now was to return the princess to the care of Amah and get himself back to the familiar routine of his chores.

He walked in the lead, looking at nothing, and saw out in front of him with the fuzziness of a fading memory the five of them back on the dunes, climbing, laughing, and talking like ordinary friends.

The only real friend he'd ever had was Little Limp, and Chengli hadn't even thought of him in weeks. Little Limp drew his thoughts to Old Cook, and his stomach began to ache. Could it be, he wondered, that Meiling loved her Amah the way he loved Old Cook? Like the mothers they didn't remember? His eyes felt uncomfortably hot. Too much sun and sand, that was all.

Thoughts of Amah and Old Cook reminded him of the jade he carried in his pouch, and the jade made him think again of his father. It was too soon to expect anyone to remember him—the far west was where they had lived—but people moved from place to place, and someone, somewhere, might recall Inspector Chao Changwon. The swaying of the camel plodding behind him rocked his thoughts in an endless rhythm. Meiling: Friend. Fourth Brother: Enemy. Father: Forgotten. Father: Remembered. Possible: Impossible. The ideas swayed, bumped, and slid to the beat of the camel's soft plodding feet.

Halfway to the caravan field, the wind came. "Oh no!" Chengli hollered to the wind. "Why have you come back to torment me? I'm doing what you want. I'm . . ."

But this wind picked up the sand and twirled it around the camel's legs, and the camel felt it. El Kalid pulled back against the lead rope, groaning and complaining. Not a spirit wind this time, for everyone felt it!

"What's wrong with you?" Chengli snapped at El Kalid. He looked up at Meiling on her padded saddle. Both her hands gripped the long hair of the camel's shaggy hump as she kept her balance against the beast's endless swaying.

"Something's bothering him. He didn't act like this earlier," Meiling called down.

"It's the wind. Look!" Chengli said, pointing to a narrow wall of sand that snaked across the path in front of him, sweeping slowly closer, inches off the ground. The sand danced higher and higher until it swirled in front of his eyes. Through the dancing sand, distant ghost flecks moved, trailed, and disappeared. Puzzled, Chengli blinked and pulled back from the wind.

Suddenly the sky darkened, and shouts sounded across the desert.

"Sandstorm! Take cover!"

"Storm?" screamed the princess. "Take cover? Under what?" She ducked her head down against El Kalid's strong neck. "There is nothing on this entire desert taller than my knee! The sand will bury us!"

Everyone dropped to the ground and pushed their animals down, too. The donkeys, horses, and camel all instinctively tucked their faces under their bodies or into the ground, covering eyes, mouth, and nostrils.

A wall of solid yellow swept toward them.

"Grab the saddle blankets!" shouted one of the soldiers. "Get down by the animals. Turn your back to the wind. Do it *now*." The howling of the wind swallowed his voice.

The wall of sand burst in an explosion of gravel lifted from the desert floor. Chengli shoved the princess down just as the hissing sheet of yellow wind tore at them—swirling, whining, full of grit.

The wind ripped at his hands and clawed his jacket. He blinked his eyes and the ground rose and fell, appearing and disappearing in front of him.

"Get in here!" A hoarse voice, barely recognizable as the princess's, called out from under the blanket. Chengli saw her lift a corner, and he dove under, pulled the blanket tight, and slammed his eyes shut. He coughed. Sand gritted between his teeth.

They waited, rocked by wind. The fine sand slid under the blanket, under his clothes, and sifted into his eyes in spite of the rag over his face.

They waited. Chengli tried not to breathe.

They waited. The howling lowered its pitch.

They waited. The screaming wind sank into silence.

A shiver.

A scratch.

The sounds of life slowly emerged out of the packed and rearranged sand.

Chengli pulled the princess out from the mound of sand that had piled over them. He laughed. Meiling cried. Sand matted both their bodies and plastered itself on both their faces. Chengli coughed to clear his throat. The princess shook her head, and sand cascaded down onto her shoulders. She looked at him and laughed through her tears.

"We're all right," she said. "We're really all right! I've survived my first sandstorm! Let's go help the others." She led the way to where the others were digging out, and together they straggled homeward toward the caravan, one behind the other.

Tired as he was, Chengli found an enormous new thought in his head: people can change! The princess—bossy, selfish, proud—for just a short time had been a friend, and now, after the storm, she'd actually helped. He wondered if changes could last, but he didn't have time to ponder the idea, for out of somewhere came a new sound, soft and distant, interrupting his thoughts.

Louder sounds, gruff and strident, demanded his attention. Ahead of them, where a black silhouette should have shown the long line of their caravan, Chengli stared. The royal soldiers pulled to a stop. El Kalid hummed in distress.

Instead of an orderly caravan, animals milled about unattended, heading out into the endless desert. Men ran back and forth screaming. Master Fong's flag lay toppled on the ground. Arrows flew. Fires burned.

"The caravan's being attacked!" the soldiers yelled at Chengli. "Robbers! They used the storm to hide their moves."

The four soldiers grabbed for their bows and arrows and shouted orders.

"Stay here," yelled one. "The fight is not over!"

"Get your animals down! All of them!" yelled another.

"Get the princess out of sight. Get her camel *down*!"

The men galloped off toward the chaos.

Scrunched down behind their animals, Chengli and the others peeked out to watch the action. He could hear the shrieks of men and animals, the zing and thud of countless arrows, but he couldn't tell which way the arrows were flying, nor who was being hit.

"You can look," Chengli called to Dakshesh. "They're too busy to notice us."

Even from the distance, they could see that the attack had been aimed at the carts of the princess. The bandits circled on their ponies, their arrows keeping away the defenders. Others crawled over the royal carts, pulling out whatever attracted them. The dowry cart lay on its side, and thieves stuffed loot into bundles, loading up their ponies. A woman—it must be Amah—could be seen riding away behind a man on horseback, her distraught voice piercing the air.

"Put me down! I must serve my princess! Let me *down*!"

No one paid attention to Amah's wails. The horse with two riders disappeared in the distant haze.

Shivering with cold and fear, Chengli waited in the growing dusk and watched until all the attackers withdrew toward the distant mountains. Dakshesh stood up and silently led the group across the gravel to their camp.

Dakshesh and his sister looked over the damage to the carts as Chengli and Fourth Brother stood in silent disbelief. The dowry cart lay toppled and empty. The cooking cart was full of smashed and scattered cookware, and Cook himself sat cringing in a corner, white as a ghost but uninjured. The princess's own red-and-gold cart lay wrecked beyond repair, a sign, thought Chengli, of the attacker's frustration at finding no princess. In revenge, the princess's driver and Amah had both been captured. Just like my father, thought Chengli. They're gone. People disappear in the desert; Old Cook said so. "No!" he yelled. "No, no, no, no!"

Looking around, he noticed a makeshift circle set up to care for the wounded. "We've got to find Master Fong and see how we can help," Chengli said as he headed for the circle. There he found the soldiers from the princess's dowry cart, wounded but still alive. Countless injured men lay collapsed in the circle, eyes wide with fear. Moving from one man to the next, Master Fong with his helper, Uncle Tao, at his side, carried bowls of precious water, torn cloth, and words of comfort. Uncle Tao knew all about medicines and ointments made from the plants he had collected, and now his knowledge was desperately needed. As best they could, the two men washed the wounds and softened small pellets of evil-smelling medicine with which they smothered each wound. Chengli bent over to help, when the voice of the princess pierced the air.

"It's all your fault!" Meiling picked her way among the wounded, coming up beside Chengli. "The emperor will be furious. My new husband will not want me now. If you hadn't gotten us permission to go to the celebration, we would have been here, and all my soldiers could have fought in the battle. And Amah, my Amah . . ." her voice tightened and rose as she realized that everything she cared about was gone. "How could you leave us with no protection?"

Chengli and Fourth Brother stood silent. Unable to talk back or defend themselves, they looked at each other and then down at the ground. For once, even Fourth Brother had no words. He dared not argue with the princess.

Behind them, Chengli could hear the voice of Master Fong as he moved through the debris, checking the wounded, giving an order here and an encouraging word there. He must have heard Meiling's hysterical voice, for he soon came forward to join them. Sand still clung to his bushy eyebrows, and blood had dried where it had spattered across his blue jacket.

"You are looking at a disaster, young lady," he said, his voice sharp with exhaustion. "For the second time on this trip, it is my men who saved your life. Had you been here, you, too, would now be a prisoner of some unknown tribe."

The princess turned her back on the master and stamped her foot.

Angry now, Master Fong kept talking. "Life is hard sometimes, very hard, and all you can do is pick up and go on. Because my men took you to the celebration, you have survived." He pointed to the remaining cooking cart. "Go to that cart with your two young servants, and think about what I say. My men have saved your life." The look on Master's face forced Meiling to obey.

Chengli, still staring at the ground, grinned. Master had called them his *men*. He didn't have long to enjoy the compliment, though. Master Fong turned to Fourth Brother and called Chengli to join them.

"The princess was given over into our care. She is in grave trouble now, with Amah gone, her driver vanished, and her soldiers wounded. You two," he nodded at Fourth Brother and Chengli, "you two now have less work, as some of your animals have been stolen and others have died tonight. You have always worked well together, so now add to your duties the safety of the princess and her two young servants. We must show our emperor that we did our best to deliver her as instructed, in spite of the dangers that surround us."

Master's words made Chengli wince, but he nodded to show that he had heard. His thoughts, however, did not agree. How could he possibly work with Fourth Brother, now that he knew about the older boy's thieving? He didn't even want to be near him, but Chengli could not explain that to Master.

Instead he stood there and shivered. The storm, the attack, and now the order to work with that thief—it was just too much. His stomach lurched, and a chill raced down his back. He shoved his hand over his mouth and bolted away to a clump of desert thorn. His stomach lurched again, and he heaved and heaved.

When there was nothing left to throw up, he kicked sand over the disgusting mess and crumpled to the ground. Tears mingled with the sand still on his face. His energy disappeared. He curled into the sand and lay still.

eight

CHENGLI LAY IN THE SAND WITH MUSCLES THAT REFUSED TO MOVE, until gradually he recovered some of his strength and recalled what Master had said on that day they had first met: Trouble we will surely have! Well, here it was. Chengli cleaned himself up as best he could and went back to the caravan, feeling only slightly sorry for himself.

As he looked at the scene before him, everything seemed brown. The sandstorm had left a layer of brown dust over people, camels, packs, clothes, everything, even thoughts. Can thoughts be brown? he wondered. They *felt* brown. Two of the princess's carts lay in ruins. Amah was gone. Meiling sat by the wreckage, silently looking at the ground. Sudarshana had her own eyes tightly closed. She hugged the princess, it seemed to Chengli, to keep them both from falling over.

He looked for Dakshesh and found him climbing over the broken cart to get into the kitchen cart. It was not damaged, and inside he found the cook cowering behind the smashed pots. He pulled the cook out from hiding, and together they hunted for anything they could find to wrap around the shivering, silent princess.

Master Fong and Uncle Tao left the wounded and picked their way over the debris to confer quietly with the royal soldiers. Then they called the five young people together.

"This is a tragedy," Master Fong said, "for you, Princess. For all of us. We will have to delay our journey until the men and beasts heal. We must all be strong to go north across the empty land. It will take about three weeks to reach the town of Hami, and the sun gets hotter every day. The hotter the sun, the slower we are forced to walk." He looked around at the men who had gathered nearby and then turned back to the princess.

"The healthy fellows will repair the wagons. The dowry cart, I fear, is beyond repair. At any rate," he shrugged, "it now holds nothing but air."

He looked at the heap of useless wreckage and rubbed his face, making the old scar shine in the fading light. "They even took the donkey."

Abdul, coming up to the group, shook his fist at the cloud of dust on the horizon. "Those fools think every caravan is their own personal supply center!"

Chengli listened and felt his own frustration grow. "We can't replace what's been stolen. Let's just move on. I want to get going! This wind that brought the sandstorm is the same wind that pulled me from Chang'an. I'm sure of it. It wants me to keep moving toward my father. In the next town or the next, I know I will find someone who knew my father."

"Your time will come," said Master Fong. "But now," the master cocked his head toward Fourth Brother and Chengli, "we all have much work to do. You will work together to care for the princess. Clean up the carts. Find a place for her to sleep."

"I can't," began Chengli, nodding his head toward Fourth Brother.

"Oh, Master," Fourth Brother interrupted, "Little Brother and I make a good team."

When did you change my name? yelled Chengli in his mind.

"We have long practice working together, Master," Fourth Brother continued. "We will do as you say." He grinned and leaned down until his nose was just a few inches from Chengli's face. Chengli had never seen him quite this close before: the eyes, brown as stone; the grin, not friendly; the hands, dropped at the wrists, floating—a reminder of the ghosts that would haunt him if he ever chose to cross the older boy. It was a small gesture holding a world of threat. Chengli's stomach muscles jerked into a knot.

Thus, for the next two weeks, Uncle Tao kept busy brewing herbs and tonics for those with fevers, and Bori the Wolf applied the mysterious stinking ointments to the open wounds of both men and beasts. Gradually people and animals healed and grew restless. Small caravans went ahead on their own, unwilling to wait for Master Fong. One chose to turn directly west and head straight out into the empty land of the Taklamakan, the desert whose very name meant "go in and you won't come out." They hoped the straight line across the desert would be a shortcut to Kashgar.

"You are fools! You will die!" Bori shouted after the departing caravan. "White dragon mounds block the way. You will find no water. None." He turned his back on them and muttered, "Go if you must, but you won't live to come out."

"We, however," Master Fong ordered, "will take the long route to the north, around the edge of the desert, stopping briefly at the town of Hami. After that, we will turn west along the base of the Tian Shan, Heavenly Mountains. That way, we will meet with the occasional rivers that flow from snowcapped peaks and bring water to each oasis."

"It will take us weeks to walk between rivers," Chengli grumbled.

"But eventually each river does appear," Master Fong said, "and with it, farms, food, water—and the towns where you can ask about your father."

Master Fong also grew more restless with each passing day, fretting as the summer heat grew intense. "To survive the heat," he said, "we will sleep during the day and walk by moonlight. Prepare. We move out at sundown."

And then the new pattern set in. Night and day were reversed. At night, the camel drivers roped themselves to their string of ten animals, and the animals each to the next, for if separated in the black of night, the nearby sand dunes became like living dragons. They reared, black against each other with a sameness that could lead any lone wanderer to a shadowy and confusing death.

Thus the nights went by, lonely and tedious, with softly jangling camel bells the only sound in the huge enveloping silence. Chengli took turns with Fourth Brother, caring for the animals and protecting the princess. When he worked alone, he could often hear her and the servants talking softly in the shadowy distance. Princess and her girl-servant had both changed into rough brown tunics and pants, better suited to walking the sandy desert. Meiling grows strong, Chengli thought. She walks more, complains less. The desert changes her.

They'd been walking now for some ten or twelve weeks—he'd lost count—but it was the end of the sixth month, and it was summer instead of spring. Bori said they were halfway to Kashgar. Halfway, thought Chengli, *only* halfway. A thousand miles behind, a thousand more in front. They survived because the nights were cool. But within an hour of sunrise, the heat soared so that even breathing became difficult. Hot air seared Chengli's nose. Dust clogged his throat. Each man found a way to build shade with makeshift tents or a blanket pulled over a camel and into the sand, and in their spot of shade, they tried to sleep. In such a way, the caravan moved north for twenty more days, until across the brown wasteland, he could see the tower signaling the gate to Hami. There was a single roof on that tower, Chengli noticed, the sign of a smaller town. As they drew nearer, the green trees and fields appeared, then the river, and finally the town of Hami rising above the flat line of the desert. Again the road followed the narrow strip of irrigated land, lush and green and enticing with the promise of melons—large oblong melons, with pale yellow skin and fruit so crisp and fragrant that hundreds were sent each year down to Chang'an for the emperor. And the emperor loved them so much that he named them after the town—the "Hami Melon." Chengli's mouth watered just thinking of them, but sadly, it was too early in the year to eat them. Master

Fong bought preserved ones and promised them fresh ones by the time they reached the next town.

Chengli stopped thinking about food as the dirt road became crowded and he had to force the camels to walk along the edge. Wooden ox carts rumbled slowly along, as farmers took newly picked vegetables to the city markets. Dogs barked, children ran, and friends called to each other as they passed. After the long weeks of the silent desert, Chengli's spirits rose, and hope rushed into his chest. He felt his heart beat faster. Finally he'd have a chance to ask about his father. Here in this town, surely someone would know of him. As the caravan stopped and settled for the day, Chengli hunted for Master Fong to ask permission to go into town.

Meiling's call interrupted him. "Skinny One," she called, "I am tired of walking in the dust of your camels. If I am to be a nomad bride, I must learn to ride a horse. You will teach me."

"Not me. I can't."

"You can't? But I order you! Remember, I can also order you separated from your head."

Chengli jumped, startled at the memory. He turned to flee, but her eyes twinkled and a smile lit up her face.

"But," Chengli said, trying to escape her demanding voice, "truly I can't. I must work." Then under his breath he added, "I don't know how to ride a horse, anyway."

"What? You are a master animal driver. You are at ease with both camels and donkeys."

"I am useless with horses. I do not understand their spirits. They are too large and too strong, and," he hesitated, "if I sit on one, I am too far from the ground!"

He looked at the ground, hoping the horse-riding soldiers were too far away to hear. He felt, for the very first time, like the skinny little one they all called him.

"And besides," he said as he looked up again, "I won't be here. I must go to the town. I must find out if anyone remembers my father."

Just then, Fourth Brother passed by on his way to breakfast. "Princess, I know how to ride a horse. I can help you." He grinned at Chengli. "Go. Take care of your work. I'll take care of the princess." His grin turned into a sneer as his lip curled scornfully.

Heat flashed across Chengli's face. He reached out to stop Meiling from following Fourth Brother but quickly dropped his hand. He watched them turn to ask the soldier for the loan of a horse. Helpless, he turned toward the town.

"Wait!" Dakshesh called out. "I have no love of horses. May I go with you? You shouldn't go alone into a strange new town."

"You would join me? It will be good to have a companion. I'd welcome your company. Two are always stronger than one."

Heading toward the town, they did their best to become presentable, brushing dust off their brown tunics and stamping their feet to clean their trousers. They fell in step with the crowd as they approached the mud-brick wall surrounding the city and passed through the arch that pierced through the massive brick platform that held the lookout tower. The gates stood open, and two useless guards dozed in the shade of the wall. The boys walked along a street of hard-packed earth in a town that looked and smelled like all the others—buildings like small, mud-brick boxes, opened to the street with vendors sitting in the openings, selling everything from bean soup to stringed instruments. Crowds pushed this way and that, making their way around stinking animal droppings and rotting garbage. Chengli's hopes began to fade. How, in this huge and unknown city with only this one day to search, could he possibly find anyone who might know about his father. He couldn't ask just anybody, for most people stayed far away from officials, fearing to be thrown into jail for something they didn't do, or forced to pay a tax for something they didn't own. Soldiers might know. A magistrate might know. But where to find them, he wondered.

That is, until they looked down a side road and saw just ahead an ornately carved, lattice gate protected by uniformed guards standing stiffly with iron trident spears at their sides. Suspecting a magistrate's office, the boys approached. The guards snapped their spears closed in an X across the walkway and glared at the boys.

"Filthy scum, be gone!" ordered the guard.

"Most honored warrior, the desert dust makes all men equal." Chengli flinched at using such honorific language to lowly guards, but it seemed the only way to get past them. He thought of Fourth Brother and tried to sound like him.

"I am nobody, but my family name is Chau and my father was Inspector Chau Changwon." He said it a bit too loudly, he knew, but he hoped that might impress the guards. "My father disappeared many years ago. I wish to talk with anyone who may know of him."

The guards relaxed their rigid stance in surprise, glancing quickly at each other. "Well, this is a unique story. Inspector Chao, eh? Who do you want to talk to?"

"I don't really know. I know only that I must talk to someone who is important enough to know an imperial inspector and has been here a long time. My father disappeared thirteen years ago."

"People come, people go . . ." the guard said disinterestedly.

"Hey, you with the crooked nose!" the second guard called to a passing worker. "Take these boys to the barracks and see if anyone out there has ever heard of Inspector Chao Changwon."

Crooked Nose slowed his pace and grumbled under his breath. He glowered at the boys and shuffled in front of them, leading them through the main courtyard, past the entrance to the magistrate's office, and back through three smaller yards until they came to the barracks, crowded with off-duty soldiers whiling away their time. Against one wall leaned the huge bows, carefully stocked arrows, and iron chariot spears that were twice as long as Chengli was tall. "No, no," he called out. "Not here. I want to talk to the magistrate."

"Start here," Crooked Nose barked. "These are the fellows who hear things. They know things." He aimed a swift kick at one sleeping man. "Wake up, Lazy Boots. Your wondrous knowledge of the world is needed." With a laugh, he turned and left the two boys standing there, waiting.

When Lazy Boots stretched himself half awake, Chengli repeated his story.

"Inspector Chao? Haven't seen him in years! Where is he these days?"

"You knew him? Really? He was killed by bandits. I'm his son, but I never knew him. That is why I'm here—looking for someone who can tell me about him."

"Everybody knew him. Everybody. Great man. Good man." Lazy Boots rambled, his voice still sleep-slurred. "Tall one. Stood out in every crowd. Loved horses. Fantastic with horses."

Lazy Boots yawned and got up off his mat. "Inspector Chao was tough. He never took a bribe. Always inspected the caravans carefully, but everyone knew he would rather be out riding horses." The man scratched his head and looked more closely at Chengli. "Who did you say you are? His son? Then you must know where he is. How is he doing now?"

"He's dead. Kidnapped," repeated Chengli in frustration. "I'm trying to learn about him, what he was like. Don't you remember anything else? Where did you last see him?"

But Lazy Boots had flopped back down on the floor, snoring loudly.

Chengli looked around the room. He rubbed the piece of jade in its pouch and then yelled out to the entire room, "Does anyone here remember my father? Family name is Chao. Personal name is Changwon. Inspector Chao Changwon. Have you even heard of him?"

Men glanced up at him, but no one moved and no one answered.

Chengli tried again. "Can I go see the magistrate? Maybe he knows!"

Lazy Boots choked on a snore and pulled himself up on one elbow. "Go away, boy. Magistrate is new here. He knows nothing about anything!"

Chengli shrugged and poked Dakshesh in the ribs. "It's no use. Let's go."

That evening, as the caravan workers busied themselves with their chores preparing for the next march, Chengli glanced up to see Fourth Brother approaching along the line of shadows. He had been working on the princess's cart, and as Chengli watched him, the older boy stooped to pick up something from the sand. As Fourth Brother crept by, the thing in his hand—a comb—caught the light from the setting sun.

Chengli squinted his eyes to make sure he had seen correctly. The comb in Fourth Brother's hand seemed unusual, with delicate teeth held in a half circle of ivory and a handle hammered in gold, barely visible in the fading light. When Fourth Brother noticed Chengli watching, the comb quickly disappeared into his pouch. Chengli shrugged—it was none of his business—and turned his thoughts back to his camels.

九
nine

THE NIGHTS REPEATED THEMSELVES OVER AND OVER. During the day, the searing heat of summer burned into Chengli's sleep, leaving him fretful and sullen. During the night, the mind-numbing sameness of the work drove away all thoughts of his father, even his friends, and left only the emptiness of keeping his animals in line. They walked along in the darkness, with moonlight flickering strange shadows across the dunes and the soft night breeze sending endless layers of sand whistling softly into ever-changing shapes.

And so the weeks dragged on, each exactly like the one before, until finally a day came when sunlight shimmered across the brown desert and bounced off a jagged line of white on the horizon.

"Tian Shan, the Heavenly Mountains," Master Fong sang out with unusual excitement, pointing to the thin line of white. "Praise be to all the mountain spirits! The mountains reach up into the heavens, and the heavenly spirits pack them with snow . . . snow . . . snow! Snow melts to water. Water fills the rivers. Praise to the spirits! Soon we

will eat juicy, sweet, delicious grapes, melons, and pears!"
Master's voice rose with his excitement, and with both arms
outstretched, he pointed toward the life-giving snow.

Uncle Tao called out, "We will turn west now to follow
along the foot of these mountains. They will be there, on our
right, guiding us all the way. Another month to Kucha . . .
more than a month beyond that to Kashgar. Always, the
mountains will be there alongside of us."

Bori came up beside Chengli. "The town of Turpan
has been known since ancient times for its grapes and," he
sighed and his voice sank, "its heat."

"Master Fong was right," complained Dakshesh to
Chengli after they'd arrived at Turpan and received
permission to explore the town. He wiped the sweat off his
face with the back of his hand and followed Chengli through
the tile-roofed gate with its heavy wooden doors and down
one stifling lane and up another. The brown mud-brick
buildings looked like those in every other town and village
they had visited along the route. The same square houses
with fronts open to the street had vendors hovering in the
doorways calling out to the passersby to stop and buy. Dry
puffs of dust rose with each footfall.

"Look here!" Chengli called as they picked their way
through the jostling crowd and turned a corner. A trellis
covered with grapevines arched completely over the road,
blocking the heat of the sun and filling the air with deep
shade and the sweet smell of ripening grapes.

"And look over there!" Dakshesh pointed. "That must
be something important, because soldiers are guarding a
very official-looking gate. That design carved into the wood

of the gate, the vines and lotus blossoms, must mean some official or magistrate! They might know about your father." He crossed over to the pair of guards, who quickly lowered their three-pronged spears into an X to block the entry.

"We just want to ask a question," Dakshesh called, keeping out of their reach. "We are looking for news of a man named Inspector Chao."

A smile spread across the gruff face of one guard. "Inspector Chao?" he answered. "Heard about him. Never met him. He was here five, maybe ten years ago. Why do you ask for him?"

Chengli crossed over the road and stood beside Dakshesh. He repeated his story, and the soldier listened intently. "Inspector Chao was rather famous around here. Our commander still talks about him," the soldier said. "Perhaps he will see you. Wait here." He turned and walked through the gate, closing it securely behind him. When he returned, he motioned to Dakshesh and Chengli, "Commander Su will speak with you. Follow me."

Chengli and Dakshesh followed the guard through the gate, along the garden path cooled by another grape arbor, and up the steps to the porch where a series of thick, cinnabar-red pillars, worn ragged and dull by time, supported the heavy, curved roof built in the same style of all important buildings in China—even though, Chengli noted, they were a thousand miles beyond the Great Wall of the Middle Kingdom.

Once inside, Chengli pushed his straggly hair back into his topknot and looked around. Ahead of him on a raised platform sat a huge, bearded official in a blue brocade robe of the finest silk, slit up the sides, revealing black silk trousers underneath. Chengli stared in surprise at the man's long white hair hanging loose far down his back, and his wispy white beard hanging equally far down his front.

From his seat behind his black lacquered desk, the commander could watch the entire room, where his officials sat on either side, also dressed in embroidered silk, with their hair worn, like their commander, loose and hanging straight down their backs. Everyone stopped working and stared as Chengli and Dakshesh entered.

Chengli dropped to his knees.

"Halt." Commander Su held up his hand. "What have we here?"

"Honorable Sir, the very sight of whom is dear to both gods and men . . ." Chengli's voice began in a soft whisper. "What gifts have you brought me?" the official interrupted.

"I have nothing . . . nothing, sir." Chengli winced. Of course, he should have approached any official laden with a pile of gifts, but he had nothing, nothing at all.

When the official's assistant realized that there were no gifts, he stepped forward to kick out Chengli.

The guard interrupted. "If it please you, sir, this is the young boy who says he is the son of Inspector Chao."

"You?" whispered Commander Su, "*You*, dressed as a camel driver, the inspector's son? Impossible! Explain yourself."

So once again, Chengli told his story, and the commander listened thoughtfully. "I didn't know the inspector had a family anywhere along the desert road," said the commander. "Government officials go wherever they are sent, and always, their families suffer for it." He flicked both hands grandly, and all the clerks returned to their work.

"Ah . . ." The commander fell silent and gazed at the ceiling, as if searching his memory. "What a horseman he was. I saw him stage a contest with a nomad Kazakh horse rider down from his mountain home. The Kazakhs are amazing horsemen and begin riding even before they can walk, yet the inspector won the contest. Beyond belief! He rode faster than their best man and made the sharp turns more tightly, racing with one hand on the horse and the other in the air. People talked about it for years. Too bad about the bandits."

Chengli's head jolted up. "Bandits, Your Honor?"

"Ah yes, bandits caused the loss of one of our best officials. Somewhere far to the west, I believe. What a waste!"

Chengli respectfully looked down again at the floor but felt his mind go in two directions at once. It was good, in a way, to know that what Old Cook in Chang'an had said was really true: his father had indeed been killed by bandits. Knowing this settled the confusion he carried in his mind. But now he also knew he'd never meet his father and would never be able to ask about the broken piece of jade he carried in his pouch. He wanted to show the commander but didn't dare—they'd call him a thief. So instead he asked, "Please, Your Honor, I've been told that my father had a circle of pale green jade with some writing on it. I often wonder about it. When you knew my father, did you ever see such a piece of jade?"

"No, that is news to me," the commander said. "I can tell you nothing about any jade. But music! That I can tell you. He loved to sing, and his favorites were the songs brought down by the nomads from the Tian Shan. He worked in the desert, but he dreamed—and sang—of the cool, green mountains. He didn't stay here long. He asked for a transfer, always going farther west. He spoke of Kucha, the next city to our west, as his favorite town, for the people there are famous for their love of music."

Chengli forgot about looking at the floor. "In another month, *we* will be in Kucha!" he exclaimed, grinning at the magistrate. Then realizing his rude behavior, he quickly looked down and added, "Looking up, I express my gratitude. Looking down, I beg your forgiveness and understanding."

A flick of Commander Su's hand told Chengli that the interview had ended. He and Dakshesh backed out of the room with their heads bowed, as was customary when leaving the presence of anyone higher up on the social scale. Chengli sighed—everyone was higher up than a camel driver.

Outside, Chengli walked along deep in thought, his body hunched forward and his hands clasped behind his back.

"You walk like an old man," teased Dakshesh.

"I feel like one," Chengli answered softly. "I always thought Father was important, but not this important. A famous horseman! A noted singer! When I knew nothing about him, I felt proud to be his son. But now I feel I'm not worthy to be his son. I can't do anything except work with camels, and I surely cannot ride a horse!"

"You might be right," Dakshesh joked, scuffing his feet to kick up a cloud of dust. "Maybe you are worthless! But I think your father's spirit must be pleased with a son who came all this way to learn about him!"

They returned to camp, picked up their dinner bowls, and headed for the group gathered by the fire. Sudarshana motioned Chengli aside. "I've got to tell you what has happened," she whispered. "Fourth Brother told Master Fong that he found a comb—a golden royal comb—on the ground next to *your* camel. It's from the princess's cart. He said you stole it."

Chengli gasped in surprise and dropped his bowl. In two leaps Chengli found Fourth Brother, grabbed hold of his topknot, and yanked him to the ground. Fists pummeling hard, Chengli yelled, "Don't you blame me! I do not steal!"

Taken by surprise, Fourth Brother twisted and rolled to face Chengli. But before he could return the blows, Master Fong shouted, "Stop! We will have no fighting! Calm yourselves!" Speaking more softly, he continued, "Chengli, we have no reason to suspect you. Go and eat."

ten

AFTER A WEEK OF REST AT THE OASIS OF TURPAN, the caravan set out once more, and Chengli had learned nothing about his father except that he could ride a horse and he loved music. It was something . . . but it wasn't much. When he thought about it at all, he thought how he was not like his father. His father was important; Chengli was nobody. His father loved horses; Chengli knew only camels and donkeys. This was not what Chengli had hoped for.

As they prepared to leave Turpan, Master realized that the sun had lost a bit of its heat, and thus the caravan returned to traveling by day. They still walked with the dry, desolate sand of the Taklamakan Desert on their left, but now they walked to the west, with the gray of the Gobi Desert far behind them. On their right, the Tian Shan mountains soared into the heavens.

Mile followed mile, week followed week, and Chengli kept scanning the horizon, hoping to see more than just the desert haze hanging low against the ground. And then the call came down the line, "Look! A shadow above the haze! It's the double roofs of the tower on the gate to Kucha!"

Even with the tower in view, they walked two more days before they could see the red brick below the tower, and even then, the view of the archway was blocked by the farms along the river. With the farms came the flocks of sheep. Tiny waterwheels lifted water from the narrow river and splashed it into irrigation ditches. Orange persimmons and red pomegranates hung ripening on their trees. Beyond the trees, finally, the crenelated stone wall of the city came into view.

Master Fong's caravan set up camp, and by the second day Chengli got his turn to explore the city.

"Are you coming?" Chengli shouted to Dakshesh and Sudarshana.

"Yes. The princess is coming, too," the girl called back.

Meiling and her royal guard rode their horses up to Chengli. "Where is Fourth Brother?" Meiling asked.

"I haven't seen him," Chengli said. "Let's go without him."

They approached the city but stopped to stare at the two huge statues of Buddha guarding the entrance, towering twice as high as the wall itself. "Trust in Buddha is strong here," said Dakshesh, and sure enough, inside the city, the streets were crowded with hundreds of brown-robed Buddhist monks mingling with the crowds by the shops, talking in small groups by the bazaar,andr standing quietly with their begging bowls held out, waiting for gifts.

Meiling and her guard gave their horses into the care of one of the monks and walked to join Chengli. He grinned and stretched his arms out wide. "This is just like being in Chang'an!" he said. "A huge city and thousands of people—

all kinds of clothes and all colors of hair. And what a jangle of words! People must come with the caravans and then decide to stay. It really is like being home in Chang'an."

"There's a difference, though," Sudarshana said. "Here it seems music comes at us from every street corner!"

Sure enough, dancers in long, colorful skirts twirled and swayed with delicate hand motions and arms that sparkled with bracelets of red, blue, and clear beads. Even their slippers glittered with the jewels sewn on. By a fountain, a man played on a two-stringed instrument that looked like a round gourd with a long handle. Down the street, two drummers strolled along pounding out powerful rhythms, and at a street corner, a group of old women stood playing four-stringed instruments, jade flutes, and a sheep-skin drum.

Dakshesh laughed. "That old woman is banging on her drum as if it were a naughty child!"

"I adore big cities," Meiling said, her voice rising with excitement. "Truly, I will rot living in a nomad camp. I cannot even imagine living in a tent and drinking tea made of rotten milk!" She gave a toss of her imperial head and led the way into the bazaar. Narrow stalls lined both sides of the walkway, where merchants sold everything from nuts and raisins to ornate daggers and bejeweled swords. Others sold hats, knives, boots, shoes, vegetables, nuts, and even carpets. Dakshesh stepped around one shopkeeper sitting on the ground, his long striped robe wrapped around his knees and dusty, bare feet sticking out from the folds. Chengli watched a merchant packing fresh eggs in a basket, each layer of eggs protected by a layer of sand.

The center of the bazaar opened into a large courtyard crowded with a haphazard collection of rough-hewn tables, wobbly benches, and food vendors selling fresh fruit right next to another selling chunks of roasted lamb or dried squid and octopus brought from the far, far oceans. Side alleys sent out the squeals and snorts of goats and sheep waiting to be traded.

"We will eat and watch the entertainment," ordered Meiling. "Choose a table at once and order some fruit for each of us." Chengli obeyed.

"Kucha is so busy, it makes Chang'an seem calm," Meiling said as she settled onto a bench. The royal guard stood behind her and accepted a pear from Chengli. "In the emperor's city, everyone lives by the emperor's rules. In Dunhuang, the city of the festivals at the dunes, soldiers and inspectors give the orders. Here, I think there must be hundreds of rules, and they are all different."

"So here we can do whatever we want!" Chengli said, sucking the sweet juice from his pear.

"I will buy a hundred ribbons and tie them all into my hair at once," Sudarshana said, running her hands across her braided hair.

"I will leave our caravan and join one headed south over the mountains, back to my family," said Dakshesh, climbing up on the bench and pretending to look over the mountains.

"I," Chengli said grandly, "will help our princess escape from the caravan so she can live forever here in the city!" He bowed low before Meiling.

"Thank you, Skinny One," Meiling said. "I accept your grand offer, and in return, I promise never again to give the order to remove your head from your shoulders!" She laughed and motioned Chengli to rise.

"Look," Sudarshana pointed left. "Dancers from . . ."

"Persia," interrupted a woman standing nearby. "They come every year." The rhythmic beating of the drums kept the dancers twirling in an uneven circle, with their left hands on their hips and left legs almost straight. Their tight-sleeved blouses and long, flowing skirts were embroidered in many colors, and at their waists they wore wide, silver belts. Their hair hung loose and flicked across their faces as they twirled.

"What fun to dance like that and let your hair hang loose!" said Sudarshana.

"And there," Meiling said, pointing straight ahead, "look at all those musicians piled onto one camel." She stared up at the six musicians who sat back to back on a platform fitted over the camel's two humps. "They play such happy music, even the camel dances to the rhythm." She recognized their song and sang along.

"Come, join us," the drummer called down to Meiling. "There's always room for one more."

"Princess," Chengli said, "you could escape your fate if you joined a group like that! They travel. No one would ever find you."

"Oh," Meiling shook her head, "I couldn't, not really." She watched as the camel swayed in time with the music. "But," she grinned and hummed another line, "what fun it must be to live like that."

"Look over *there*," Chengli nodded to a shadowy group of men hovering together over one filthy table, their daggers glinting in the sunlight. "Cutthroats and thieves, I'm sure. Keep them away from me!"

"But," Dakshesh exclaimed, "that's Fourth Brother there right in the middle of them."

"He's probably trying to sell something," Chengli grumbled, just as the musicians' camel bumped its way between the tables, blocking his view.

"Fight! Fight!" Shouts filled the courtyard. The royal guard jumped forward, pushing Meiling down under the table.

Dakshesh leaped up on the table. "Fourth Brother's right in the middle of the fight!" he yelled.

"Fourth Brother, come out of there right now!" shrieked Meiling as she scrambled out from under the table, trying to see.

Men ran from all directions, elbowing their way into the fight. Fourth Brother disappeared.

"Find him!" Meiling shouted.

Chengli scrambled over the table and shoved his way into the thrashing tangle of arms and elbows. He ducked one blow and darted between two others, but he didn't see Fourth Brother anywhere.

The fight spread across the courtyard. Chairs toppled. The musicians' camel bolted. Musicians tumbled, instruments fell, and Chengli fought his way back through the mess to Sudarshana and Dakshesh. "We better get out of here!" he yelled.

Meiling's chair was empty. "Where's the princess? Where's the guard?"

Sudarshana looked around wildly. "Under the table!" she screamed. "The guard is under the table. There's blood all over his face. Where's Meiling?"

"There!" Dakshesh pointed across the yard to the archway that led out of the bazaar.

Chengli swung around just in time to see a man carrying Meiling, kicking and screaming, out through the gate.

"Stop him!" Chengli yelled to anyone within earshot. "He's got our princess! Somebody do something!"

His cries slid unnoticed into the chaos. He stood frozen in confusion, as his thoughts raced from Meiling to the wounded soldier still under the table and back to Meiling. Suddenly he yelled, "Go! Go!" and his body flew into action. Far ahead at the archway he saw the man holding Meiling push through the crowd of people and jump onto a waiting horse.

Chengli ran until he recognized the royal guard's powerful horse tied to a post. He stopped. His breath locked in his throat. I can't do this, he thought. I can't get on that animal. I can't ride horses. He shook his head and gasped for breath. His eyes clamped shut. Then he heard clearly in his head the words about his father . . . loved horses . . . powerful rider. "I will!" he shouted. "I am my father's son!" And he pulled himself up onto the back of the horse.

"Go!" he shouted, and the horse took off. Chengli dug his knees into the horse's side and hung on to its mane with all his strength. "Go, go, go!" he shouted again, and the horse strained forward to follow the trail of dust leading toward the distant mountain.

eleven

CHENGLI'S HEART POUNDED IN HIS EARS, and each of his bones jammed against its neighbor. Paralyzed with fear, he hung on, with one phrase bouncing over and over in his head: . . . help me, Father . . . help me, Father . . . help me, Father. His face tight against the horse's neck, he slipped and slid across the horse's broad back but kept his balance.

"Go faster!" yelled Chengli, and the horse strained to obey. The frantic galloping settled into its own rhythm, and Chengli stared ahead at the dust cloud that marked the wake of the princess and her captor. He watched it reach the line where the flat desert floor joined with the mountains. His horse began to close the gap that kept him from Meiling.

Then suddenly the flat, predictable desert became steep, unfamiliar land, and the horse slowed its pace.

"Hurry!" urged Chengli, but the horse slowed to pick its way between boulders and over loose stones, its hooves clacking as it struggled to find footing. Soon the forest loomed ahead, and Chengli dodged one way and the other to escape low-hanging branches. Rounding a corner, he nearly crashed into a torrent of water blocking their way, cascading wildly over rocks and fallen trees.

"Go!" shouted Chengli.

The horse stepped into the roiling water, slipped on the wet stones and reared up in terror. Chengli screamed and slid from the horse's back into the water, twisting away from the thrashing hooves.

"Aiii!" he sputtered as the freezing water cut through his thin tunic, and his foot jammed between two water-slick rocks.

"Oh, no!" He watched a pool of dark red spread from his leg into the water.

With an effort, he shoved at the heavy rocks and freed his trapped foot. He gritted his teeth and hoisted himself out of the creek. A jagged cut pulled the skin away from the front of his leg, and blood poured down over his foot. Yanking off his tunic, he hurriedly wrapped it around his leg to make a bandage. Shivering so hard he could barely move, he inched toward a spot where sunlight broke through the trees, and he sat, holding the tunic in place. Gradually the blood stopped oozing. In the warmth of the sun his shivering slowed. He looked up. The horse!

Where was the horse?

He looked up the mountain. He looked down the way he had come. As far as he could see, there was no horse. Only trees, stones, and the sound of thundering water. However was he going to find Meiling without a horse to ride?

He hugged his injured leg and sat in a trance as the sunlight shifted out of sight behind the trees. Warmth drained away and shadows deepened. In his misery, the shadows of the tall spruce trees played tricks on his mind, and the branches curved out and up, not trees at all, but the wide tiled eaves of the Chang'an city gate curving up to the heavens.

"Now what?" he asked himself. I have to get through the night, he thought. He was so useless! He'd lost the princess, lost the horse, and ripped open his leg. He was cold and wet and hungry, and there was not a thing he could do about it. Plus his leg hurt worse every minute.

He pulled himself into a tight ball and tried to stay warm. "I am too old to cry," he yelled out loud. The sound of his own voice helped him feel less alone, and he rubbed his fists across his eyes.

To avoid freezing in the autumn night, he had to find a way to keep warm. He pulled himself toward some boulders clumped together and wondered how cold stone could provide shelter from the wind. Some fallen branches thick with rough spruce needles helped, but the cones poked at his sore body. He pulled them off. "Now," he mumbled, "I've just got to wait for morning."

Exhausted, he slept.

Sunlight warmed his body. He rolled over, opened his eyes, and cringed. A dagger glinted in the sunlight, its tip right under his nose!

He slammed his eyes shut, then slowly opened them again. The dagger still quivered near his throat. He kept his head motionless and looked at the drawn dagger, then to the hand that held it, and slowly up to the face. Fierce eyes glinted at him above a huge, bulbous nose with tufts of ugly nose hair poking out. Chengli decided he did not like that face.

He glanced sideways. Two other men, with muscles bulging like wrestlers, knelt there, daggers ready. Their eyes glared wildly, and hair stuck out all over their heads. Brushes of hair hid their upper lips, and more hair like mops covered their chins. No man from the Middle Kingdom would hide his face like this. Who were these strangers?

"Please," Chengli thought he'd better say something, and it had better be polite, just in case they spoke his language—he had heard of the many nomad groups that lived in these mountains, all speaking different languages. "Please, I'm just a lost boy." His voice squeaked; he tried again. "I'm not dangerous! Truly, you don't need your daggers!" He watched, but the daggers didn't move.

The men talked loudly among themselves, in a language Chengli didn't recognize, their voices gruff and sharp. They got up and searched behind the trees. Chengli waited. When they seemed to agree that he was alone and helpless, they sheathed their daggers.

One man—taller than the others—reached over and yanked up Chengli from his bed of spruce needles. Chengli screamed in pain and grabbed at his leg. The man noticed the makeshift bandage around the wounded leg and yanked it off. The wound had dried tight against the cloth and now the bleeding began again. The man shoved the tunic back in place and pulled the sleeves forward to tie it snugly against Chengli's leg.

A sharp whistle from one of the men brought three horses out of the forest. The leader picked up Chengli as if he weighed nothing at all and set him on a horse, mounting behind him. The group set off up the mountain, the men talking and laughing as they rode along.

Chengli kept watching these wild warriors. What will they do with me? he wondered as he bounced along. Where are we going? He knew he should be frightened, but he wasn't. Anything was better than sitting cold, hungry, and completely alone with a leg that screamed for attention.

The throbbing in his leg kept rhythm with the horse's stride. Up they went, through a break in the mountain wall, down a gorge, and out onto a high mountain meadow. A settlement of a dozen nomad yurts—round tents covered with layers of pounded sheep's wool—came into view.

His captors rode up to the front of one yurt, and the leader grinned happily and burst into song.

A song? thought Chengli. I'm miserable, and he sings about it?

The song apparently announced their arrival, for someone pulled back the cloth flap that served as a door. Out came what appeared be the mother, father, then grandfather, and a young boy who also had wild, bushy hair. They circled around Chengli, pointing, laughing, and poking at Chengli's bare skin, as if he were some strange unknown animal purchased down at the desert bazaar. Friend or foe? wondered Chengli through the haze of his pain. Cruel or just curious? Bandits or shepherds?

The mother noticed Chengli's leg. Her tone changed, and without understanding her words, Chengli sensed she would take care of him. He moved to get down off the horse. The world swayed and blurred. Then all went black.

He awoke inside the yurt dressed in a clean, warm tunic and covered by a soft, woolen blanket. His leg felt strange—it stung but no longer throbbed. He sat up and looked around. First he checked his leg and found it wrapped in a soft, clean cloth. He poked beneath the cloth and discovered slices of fresh onion bound snugly against the cut. So that's what makes it sting! Now he knew one thing: the mother was friendly. She had given him clothes, a bed, and even taken care of his leg—doing it all while he slept.

Encouraged by the care he'd been given, he pulled off the blanket and swung his legs off the sleeping mat. A searing pain shot up his wounded leg! He gasped and slowly eased himself back down under the blanket. Staying totally motionless, the pain gradually subsided. I won't try that again for awhile, thought Chengli.

He looked around the tent. Thick carpets of red and yellow covered the floor and much of the walls. Bright, embroidered cushions served as chairs. Orange and yellow ribbons draped and crisscrossed behind the wooden spokes that held up the tent. After months on the desert, the bright colors made Chengli blink.

A small fire burned in the stone circle at the center of the tent. Thin threads of white smoke circled the room and made their way out through the smoke-hole in the roof. On the fire, a simmering pot sent out a new and inviting smell. It seemed like a long, long time since he'd had anything to eat.

Voices outside warned Chengli that the family had returned. One by one, they came in through the flap that served as a door, looked at him, and then sat around the fire. Each one said something to Chengli, and he tried to look friendly in return.

The son, the one with the wild bushy hair, looked straight at Chengli, his smile twisting into a smirk. "So," he said, "you fell off horse!"

Chengli felt the smile leave his face and his eyes widen in surprise. He nodded.

"Surprised I speak your language?" asked the boy. "I Agha. I go down to the bazaar. I learn."

Chengli watched and waited.

Agha leaned over Chengli's mat. "Only babies fall off horses. Don't know how to ride?" he taunted.

Chengli's surprise edged close to anger.

The family around the fire called to Agha to join them, and Chengli relaxed. Bowls of hot stew were passed to each person, and one was handed to Chengli. Before he could begin eating, the mother spoke. Agha turned back to Chengli.

"Mother asks why you here. Boy from Middle Kingdom in high mountain Kazakh grazing land—it never happen before. People from Middle Kingdom not visit nomad families."

"It's a long story," Chengli said. "Most important, I am alone, and I am not dangerous. I tried something," he sighed and looked around the room, "and I failed. I lost my caravan. I lost my princess. And I lost my horse. I have no idea what to do next."

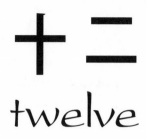

twelve

CHENGLI LAY BACK ON HIS MAT and drifted in and out of the life around him. He thought one day had passed, or maybe three or four. He wasn't sure. The pain pierced through his leg and tugged at his entire body so that he thought he might never walk again.

The men ignored him, but the mother brought him food and changed the bandage over his wound, placing fresh onion slices on it to keep the angry demons away. She seemed as tall and strong as the men in the family, but it was her hair that fascinated Chengli—it hung to her waist in six or seven long braids, but it never seemed to get in her way as she worked. Chengli liked her gentle smile—and she smiled often. Her clear brown eyes had a soft look that invited Chengli to talk. What a pleasure that would be, but without words he could only return the smile. She talked constantly, as if somehow Chengli would understand.

"Mother has decide, and no one can argue," said Agha one morning. "You our guest until leg has healed."

"And then?" asked Chengli, sitting up on his mat.

"Then family decide what to do." Agha shrugged.

"Do? You don't have to *do* anything," Chengli said in surprise. "I don't *want* to stay here." He looked around the tent, then back at Agha. "But I don't know how I'll leave, either. I have no horse and nowhere to go. The caravan has surely already left Kucha without me. And besides, I have to rescue the princess."

"Not very good plan," Agha said as he put on his jacket and a hat topped with eagle feathers. He turned away to wrap his left arm in layers of heavy, padded leather. Chengli recognized the sign that Agha planned to go hunting with his eagle. There would be fresh meat for supper. He admired Agha, but he didn't like him. Agha had a way of making everything he said sound like an insult. He seemed a little younger than Chengli, and he had the same curly, short hair as the rest of his family—in fact, like all the rest of the families in this meadow of nomads. He had skills that Chengli had never seen, especially the hunting—not with a bow and arrow, but with an eagle.

Through the open tent flap, Chengli watched Agha, barefoot and balancing on his horse without a saddle, release the blindfolded eagle from its wooden perch. As it rode on Agha's padded arm, it stretched out its powerful wings and nearly knocked Agha off his horse.

"I've got to get out of here," Chengli grumbled, "but how?" He clenched his teeth to help himself concentrate. He had learned the silk trade for his Chang'an merchant and then learned how to service a caravan trade for Master Fong. None of that helped him now. Here on the mountain, surrounded by lush green meadows and towering spruce trees, he felt ignorant and helpless. He pounded his fist against his forehead, as if to pound in some useful thoughts.

What do I know from my other lives that can be useful here in these mountains? What do I know that will help me find Meiling? he wondered glumly. He sat gazing at the orange and yellow ribbons that threaded their way around the poles of the tent. Not a thing, he decided. Not a thing!

But he knew that he could do nothing at all until his leg healed, so he pulled himself up and tried to walk around inside the tent. The pain made him wince, but he could do it.

At the end of the week, Mother made him a crutch from a tree branch, put boots of soft padded leather on his feet, and sent him out into the sunshine.

The wind welcomed him, brushing against his face with a dance of autumn crispness. This was not the dry, wailing wind of the desert. This breeze came heavy with the aroma of fields and meadows and forests beyond.

He limped along the edge of the settlement, thankful for his tree-branch crutch. Three or four camels lay contentedly in the grass. Sheep munched their way around the tents and soon became his friends, following him and crowding him, nuzzling his side, almost asking him to pat their soft, black-and-white wool. It was peaceful here, but he didn't feel peaceful. He had to find Meiling. Where could she be? And how could he ever find her, with no horse to take him anywhere at all!

Across the settlement, a song interrupted his thoughts. He grinned. Something important must have happened, because these mountain people announced every bit of news with music.

"Well, boy, hear music?" The old grandfather, White Beard—he must have had a name, but he was called White Beard by everyone to acknowledge that he had lived long and grown wise—appeared out of the forest with a load of wood balanced on his shoulders. He walked slowly, his long robe of green-and-tan stripes flopping gently against his legs, and his feet protected by thick, padded boots.

"Greetings, Grandfather! Yes, I hear it." Chengli answered. "Do you know what has happened?"

"Hojanias, our eldest son," White Beard said. "Home from Kucha." White Beard shifted his load and kept walking across the meadow. "He wants meet you."

"White Beard," Chengli said, suddenly realizing that he understood the words, "you speak the language of the Middle Kingdom! I didn't know."

"Little bit, boy, and very bad. I forget much," White Beard chuckled. He dropped his load of wood and looked kindly at Chengli. "When you well again, boy, what you want?" White Beard's bushy white eyebrows pushed together above his nose. The skin around his dark eyes crinkled as he smiled at Chengli.

"What do I want?" echoed Chengli.

"Why come to mountain?" White Beard's voice, soft and encouraging, drew out the story once more.

In simple sentences, Chengli explained about the princess, how she had been kidnapped, and how he hoped to find and rescue her.

"What plan, boy?" asked White Beard, sitting down on the pile of wood, straightening his long robe, and looking carefully at Chengli.

"Plan? I have no plan, Grandfather. I don't know where she is. I don't know how to find her. I don't know what to do if I *do* find her." Chengli watched White Beard, and for several seconds he felt the old man's eyes searching deep into his own.

"Not good, boy. Get plan," White Beard said, breaking the silence. He stood up, turned up the collar of his robe against the chill in the air, and heaved the wood back onto his shoulders. "Come. Walk. Make plan."

Chengli limped along beside the grandfather and tried to think. So far, he had never made a plan. Things just happened. He had never thought out a plan to *make* things happen.

"I don't think I know how to make a plan," Chengli admitted, leaning on his crutch.

"What you want?"

"The princess."

"Why?"

"Because I'm the one who came up with such great ideas to change her life." Chengli's thoughts began to tumble out. He forgot to keep the words simple so that White Beard could understand. "They were just ideas, those things we talked about, like how she could run away and join the singers down in Kucha. But ideas turn into wishes, and the spirits heard the wishes and made them happen. Now her life *has* changed, and it's all my fault. So," he turned and looked at White Beard, "I'm the one who should find her."

A shout caused Chengli to turn. Across the meadow bounded Hojanias, swatting at the sheep that blocked his way.

"Hojanias, welcome," White Beard called. "Come. Tell news from the desert."

Hojanias ran up, tall and strong, with the same curly hair as his younger brother, Agha, but with eyes that sparkled with gentle friendship. Chengli liked him immediately.

"I've been away," he said, looking at Chengli and the crutch, "but I know all about you. I go to Kucha often to trade furs for food." Hojanias lifted Chengli right off the ground and spun him around in a dizzying circle. "You're awfully young to be the cause of all the talk."

Down on the ground again, Chengli steadied himself with his crutch. "What do you mean, all the talk?" he asked.

"It's quite the news down in the bazaar," Hojanias said, clapping Chengli on the shoulder. "What a story. The best we've heard in years! You're famous, boy. How an imperial royal princess and a lowly caravan boy both disappeared on the same night! People argue all over Kucha."

Chengli stared at Hojanias. "Argue? Why should they argue?"

"Well, some say they *saw* bandits kidnap the princess, and a boy—that must be you—ride off on a horse to save her."

"There's no argument," Chengli said, hopping around his crutch. "That's what happened."

"Oh, but there *is* argument," Hojanias continued. "Others say they heard, actually *heard*, the same boy planning to help the royal princess escape, and that's what happened. He helped her escape!" Hojanias landed a playful punch on Chengli's back. "What a nest of bumblebees you have made down in Kucha."

He laughed, threw his arms out wide, and called to the wind. "Our little guest is famous!"

"Hojanias, tell me," Chengli asked. "Did you hear anything

about my caravan or my caravan master, Master Fong?"

"He has completely vanished—gone into hiding! They say he is terrified to show up at either end of his route—Kashgar or Chang'an. He has lost a royal princess, and the emperor's men would slice him in two at the waist for such a crime! Only an idiot would stay with the caravan now." Hojanias jumped over a fallen tree trunk and stood before Chengli. "But even without Master Fong, or you, or the princess, the caravan is moving west to reach their final stop at the city of Kashgar, for it is there that they will sell their loads to merchants from the far distant lands. I saw your caravan leave before I started for home."

Chengli grabbed at Hojanias and caught hold of his brightly embroidered vest. "Now you see," he said, his voice strong and pleading, "I must find Meiling and take her back. I knew I had to save her, but now I must save my master, also. If I take her back to the caravan, they will both be safe!" He stopped and looked from White Beard to Hojanias. "I must go! Now!"

Hojanias rubbed his hands through his hair and turned to Grandfather. "With your permission, I will go and pass the word around this village, so that anyone who travels will keep asking, and we will wait for news of your princess. News spreads slowly across these high mountains," he said, "but it does spread. People travel back and forth, following their sheep, trading their wares, visiting relatives—and always sharing the latest news."

And indeed, before another week had ended, a stranger rode into the valley, reined his horse to a stop in front of White Beard's yurt, and burst into song:

"I have news, good news, bad news.
Good—your princess we have seen.
Bad—she is a prisoner of Haza the bandit.
Heading west, farther west.
Not north, not south, always west."

"Come on, boy, your leg has almost completely healed. Get rid of your crutch, and let's go get your princess!" yelled Hojanias. "I'll go with you. We'll take two horses—one for me, one for you. We'll go to my uncle's village and wait there for more news. I'll give you to my cousins, and they will take you farther on your journey." He turned but yelled over his shoulder, "Get your things. Let's go!"

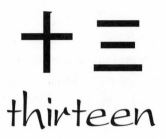

thirteen

HOJANIAS RETURNED TO CHENGLI riding his light gray horse and leading a dark brown one. Behind each saddle, he had fastened a leather pouch. Chengli stood waiting, holding his small pile of caravan clothes, his only possession.

"Caravan Boy!" Mother called. She ran out from the yurt, talking all the while and tugging at Chengli's pile of clothes, taking them and stuffing them into the travel pouch. Then she turned him around and made him put on a coat of black-and-tan stripes and new tall boots of soft, padded leather. She pushed onto his head a hat with two flaps that could be rolled down over his ears when the weather turned cold. Fox fur lined the entire hat.

She stepped back, hands on hips, and grinned at Chengli. Hojanias nodded his approval, his uncombed hair bouncing in rhythm. "Except for your long hair pulled up in its topknot," he said, "you can now pass as my younger brother."

White Beard, followed by three of the sheep, came from behind the yurt and raised his arm in blessing. "Ride with the power of eagles" sounded in Chengli's ears as he mounted and followed Hojanias from the settlement.

"Hojanias," Chengli called ahead as their horses headed up the mountain, "I'm going to miss the sheep, but I really don't like horses."

"Don't worry, Caravan Boy. I'll teach you as we go. Soon you will ride like Kazakh-born mountain boy!"

Day after day, they made their way westward. Even without heavily loaded camels, their progress was slow. They never went over level ground—there wasn't any! They rode up one mountainside and down another, out over rolling meadows and then through a deep forest. Everything was new to Chengli . Hojanias rode beside Chengli, teaching him to ride while yelling directions and encouragement. Hojanias taught him to relax in the saddle, to go limp and let his body shake up and down like a pea on a drum. It felt strange, but Chengli's muscles stopped aching.

Gradually Chengli gained confidence and lost his fear of the horse. The rough, mountain terrain held no more surprises. At night he and Hojanias slept wrapped in their blankets, and during the day they moved slowly westward.

"Once we get over that distant ridge," called Hojanias, "we will be at the next settlement." He stopped his horse and turned to face Chengli. "They are the relatives of my mother, and I will leave you with them. I will return home. My cousin Tokta will take you farther west. I'll miss you, Caravan Boy."

Chengli gazed at Hojanias. He understood he was to be handed over to someone new at each settlement, and they would guide him on to the next, over and over, but he didn't like the idea. He kicked his horse and trotted ahead, turning his back on Hojanias. "I don't want to be with new people all the time," he yelled over his shoulder. "I'll have to explain about the princess over and over and over." He rode his horse in circles, fuming under his breath. Suddenly he turned and rode back to Hojanias. "Do they know I am coming?" he asked.

"Of course. News travels, you know," Hojanias said.

"I don't want . . ." Chengli looked away and kicked at his horse again. "Never mind," he called out. "Come on, let's go."

The next valley opened before them, but instead of a settlement, they saw only one single yurt sitting in a clearing surrounded by towering trees. Two grazing cows, a barking dog, and a horse tied to a tree were the only signs of life. But as they rode into the clearing, a tall, energetic bear of a man came running out to greet them.

"Welcome, Caravan Boy! I am Tokta. My family has moved down mountain for the winter, and I alone stayed to greet you. I have news for you." He grabbed Hojanias and held him at arms' length. "You've grown old, Cousin," he roared. He then turned to grab Chengli. "And you, Caravan Boy, look young enough for Haza the bandit to eat in one bite!"

Chengli pulled back, but Tokta slapped his thighs and laughed loudly at his own joke.

"What is your news, Cousin?" Hojanias asked.

Tokta immediately turned serious. "The band that you look for has camped for the winter near the trade route that comes up from the desert city of Kashgar, over these mountains and down into the northern flat lands," he said. "They have more than one prisoner. I am not sure what that means, but I've been thinking that this is one adventure I don't want to miss." Tokta clenched his fists, swung around, and began playfully pummeling his cousin. "Think of it! A caravan boy will try to outwit Haza, king of the bandits!"

"Are you sure you want to be there?" Chengli asked. He grinned as he watched Tokta's frantic fist fight. "Do you want to watch them carve me up and eat me for dinner?"

"Now we must be serious, boy." Tokta's voice calmed, and he looked down at Chengli. "Haza is a dangerous enemy. He is famous for his daring. He is the only one I know who would dare steal a royal princess."

"Cousin," Hojanias interrupted, looking at Tokta, "your idea is a good one—staying with our Caravan Boy, I mean. We can joke about Haza while we are far from him, but when we get near, it won't be a joke. I, too, think this is an adventure to be remembered. I am not needed at home during the winter. Let us both stay with our caravan boy and see who will win this contest!"

Thinking often of the powerful bandit, Haza, and what he might do once they met up with him, Chengli rode with Tokta and Hojanias westward through the Heavenly Mountains. Mile after mile fell behind them, and still they rode westward. Every few days they reached a new settlement, and always someone had a bit of news to guide them closer to Haza.

And then one night as they slept, autumn abruptly turned into winter. Snow fell all through the night—and the next and the next. Snow hid the paths, and winds whistled down the gullies, pushing through the forests. Chengli and his friends struggled through snow drifts and slid across frozen streams. When raging storms blocked their travel, they stayed snug in friendly yurts for days—or weeks. Chengli complained to the mountain spirits that kept the nights long and dark and the days filled with blinding snow. He paced back and forth in the small circle of the yurt.

"We will lose her if we stay here any longer," he grumbled.

He tried to help with winter chores, but every task was interrupted by his complaints about the enforced wait.

"We cannot travel in this weather," said Hojanias, "but neither can Haza. Calm your thoughts, Caravan Boy."

Chengli listened but kept on prodding them to continue with their search. Hojanias finally lost his patience. "Silence! Your persistence is beating against my head and giving me a headache!"

Chengli swallowed his eagerness and apologized. "It's no use, is it, hammering against the weather?"

He set himself to work, bending soft branches and tying them into snowshoes. He whittled at stakes that would hold up a new tent. But every day he thought about Meiling, or Haza, or both.

Finally the approaching spring warmed the air. The blanket of snow retreated into patches, and Hojanias agreed it was time to move on. The second day on the trail, a rider came toward them. Chengli gasped. A brightly colored jacket lay fastened across the back of the man's saddle.

"Look!" Chengli whispered to Hojanias, "That's Master Fong's jacket, the one with the scorpions on it! Hojanias, it's from my caravan!"

Hojanias motioned for Chengli to be quiet and turned his attention to the approaching rider.

The stranger spoke first. "News has reached us that you will not want to hear," he said. "Haza's band will host the annual spring gathering of all the nomads. The families are eager to come together. They have much to barter, trade, and much news to share. It's Haza's turn this year to be the host, and, bandit though he is, he is no threat to his own people. This may be good for you, for the gathering will force Haza to stay in one place long enough for you to catch up with him. But when it's over, he plans to head north over the mountains to sell his prisoners in a northern land where no one will recognize them or try to save them."

"Sell them?" Chengli burst out. "My princess came from the great imperial palace. She cannot live—I know she cannot live—if she is someone's slave!" Chengli turned from the messenger to Tokta. "Let's go!" he begged. "I've got to find her." He yanked on the reins, and his horse reared up.

"No!" yelled Hojanias. "Stop!"

Chengli felt the muscles in his face pull into knots. "I can't wait," he cried. "I've got to find her before it's too late!"

Hojanias reached out and caught hold of Chengli's horse.

"Caravan Boy, if you move without thought, you, too, will be a prisoner of Haza. Think first!"

Chengli didn't want to listen, but Hojanias's grip left him no choice. He rode beside Hojanias and slowly grew calm.

"What will you do?" asked Tokta, "just ride in there and say, 'I've come for the princess'? To go without a plan is not brave. It is reckless and foolish."

Chengli didn't answer.

When they stopped that evening to make camp, Chengli remembered the stranger's words. "What's a gathering?" he asked.

"The clans get together to trade things and hear the latest news," answered Tokta. "It's a time of seeing friends and relatives. There will be crowds of people, hundreds of them, with their horses and their children. There will even be a horse race for the young people."

"For the men, there will be a contest on horseback, the Dispute of the Goat," said Hojanias. "The skin of a dead goat is stuffed with straw, and each man tries to capture the goat and carry it to the flag."

"The game needs many riders," said Tokta, "and no one wants the game to end. They will grab the goat and never let it get near a flag! They tackle, grab, beat, and swing from one horse to another, back and forth, till men and horses are all exhausted."

Chengli listened and tried to imagine the excitement. "It will be hard, in the crowd," he said, "to find my princess. White Beard said I must have a plan, but I think and think, and still I have no plan."

"Wait, Caravan Boy," Tokta advised. "Wait until you see the valley and the people. Some plan will come to you."

"I've been thinking," Chengli said. "If we get all this news about Haza, doesn't he get news about me?"

"Probably."

"What will he do?"

"He will laugh, Caravan Boy," Tokta said as he poked at the campfire. "He will say, 'What can one caravan boy do against Haza the Great?'"

Chengli looked at Tokta.

Tokta looked at the fire.

"Then what?" Chengli asked.

Tokta sat silently, and then he opened his large palms, looking puzzled. "I don't know."

Chengli sat fidgeting as the silence lengthened. "Maybe," he said, "maybe Haza won't recognize me. He will watch for a boy from the Middle Kingdom. I dress like a Kazakh. I ride like a Kazakh."

"You still have long hair tied on top of your head like all the men of the Middle Kingdom. That will give you away."

"Then cut it off." Chengli reached up and untied his top knot. His long hair fell below his shoulders.

"Now?"

"Now."

Tokta reached for his dagger and chopped at Chengli's hair, fluffing it to match the short, tangled curls of Hojanias. "Now you are no longer Caravan Boy; you are our little brother!"

"And I am ready for Haza. Let's go!"

Hojanias nodded. "But first, before we get our blankets, I have something for you." He went to his pack and pulled out a bundle. "Here," he said. "Return this to your master when you see him again!"

"His jacket? How did you get his jacket?" Chengli grabbed the jacket and faced Hojanias. This jacket had been tied to the stranger's horse. Either Hojanias had bought it—not very likely—or somehow he had stolen it right off the horse. They think stealing is a game, Chengli thought, but stealing is just wrong!

"Why couldn't you bargain for it?" Chengli asked. "Why did you have to steal?" He stamped his foot and accidentally smashed his toe against a log. Kicking the log out of his way, he threw Master Fong's jacket onto the ground. "I don't want this!" he hissed. "I didn't steal in the desert, and I won't steal now!" His voice rose and cracked. He banged his fists against Tokta's chest, harder and harder. "I lost my best friend because I wouldn't steal with him." His fists kept pounding. "My father was an inspector," he gasped, "an *honest* inspector. He never stole anything—anything!"

His fists stopped pounding and locked around Tokta's belt. He peered into Tokta's dark eyes and screamed, "I am his *son*."

With a sob, Chengli let go of Tokta's belt and sat down hard on the ground. He tightened his lips and stared at his own feet. No one moved. The campfire flickered.

"Well, you are a strange one," Tokta said calmly as he picked up the jacket. "It is something to think about before you find your princess. If you take from someone a thing they took from someone else, are you stealing . . . or rescuing it to give it back? Think what has happened to the jacket. Someone stole it. Then they sold it. Then I took it. I took it from someone who shouldn't have had it, to return it to its original owner. You say that I stole it . . . and if it bothers you so much, you must think more deeply about your princess. When you find her, will you be rescuing her . . . or stealing her from Haza, who now owns her?" He paused to let his words sink in.

"You'll need to know your answer before you find your princess."

十四

fourteen

"THERE IT IS," CALLED HOJANIAS just three days later, "the valley of your missing princess!" He sat on his horse at the crest of a ridge and pointed down through the dark green branches of the spruce trees.

Chengli rode up beside him. "It's huge!" he gasped.

Far below stretched a wide valley green with the early burst of spring, and through the valley rushed a stream, swollen by melting snow. All across the valley lay a confusion of brown tents, gray yurts, and colorful carpets laid out on the grass. Around the dwelling places, Chengli could see short, stocky horses, brown camels, black-and-white sheep, and men, women, and children all dressed in a rainbow of colors.

"I never imagined so many people," Chengli said in awe.

"Hundreds," laughed Hojanias. "Ten times that, maybe."

"Come on," yelled Tokta with his usual enthusiasm, "let's go!" His horse plummeted down the mountainside, and Chengli followed as bravely as he could. Down the hill and across the valley they rode, into the jumbled collection of tents. He tried to copy the friendly gestures of the cousins as they waved and called greetings to the men and women they passed.

"Somewhere here we will find more cousins. We will stay in their tent," Hojanias called as he rode on ahead.

"Somewhere here," Tokta said with a sneer in his voice, "we will find the tent of Haza, our *gracious* host. And when we do, Little Brother, your plan must be ready."

Chengli rode behind Hojanias and Tokta as they threaded their way between animals, people, and tents. They found their aunt's tent, greeted her from horseback, and continued exploring. Children barely old enough to walk already rode well on horseback. Chengli watched the men bargain to trade fur from the mountains for pots and pans from the towns, warm fox-fur boots for the spices to season their food. And the food! From all around came the nose-tingling smell of cook fires baking the onion-covered flat bread, simmering pots of lamb stew, and roasting whole lambs.

Chengli rode out to the edge of the crowded valley, turned, and rode back along the bank of the stream. How would he recognize Haza? How could he find him in this crowd?

He rode, looking for some sign of the princess. He pushed through the crowd, greeting friends he remembered from his journey across the mountains, trying his best to look and act like all the other Kazakh boys. And always, he looked ahead, watching, listening, hoping for a clue.

Suddenly, off to the side, he saw it: a flash of brown among the brightly embroidered colors of Kazakh clothing.

He edged his horse around to watch.

Sure enough, there it was again. Two children dressed in drab brown tunics struggled to carry heavy buckets of water from the swiftly flowing river.

"Child," Chengli called, using the gruff Kazakh words he had learned, "I'm thirsty. Give some drink to a stranger."

He rode slowly up to the girl and leaned down from his saddle to scoop up water. He thanked her but sat up disappointed. She was not Meiling.

The other girl glanced up at him, her tired eyes blinking wide in recognition.

"Here," she whispered, lifting up the pail, "I can give you a drink."

Chengli stared at the bent body and rough, chapped hands. The voice was Meiling's. He started to speak, but as he opened his mouth he saw danger behind her. In the door of the tent stood a tall, bald-headed man in knee-high fur boots and a rough, woolen jacket. He didn't look dangerous, but Chengli knew immediately that he must be the dreaded Haza.

Thinking quickly, Chengli spoke up.

"Thank you, girl, but that water must go to your master!" he said, cocking his head toward the tent. In a whisper he added, "Do not show that you know me. But pay attention. I will come for you."

For the next several days, families continued to arrive in the valley. Chengli spent the time visiting, making plans, and trying to act brave and eager for the race.

"How do I enter the race?" he asked Tokta.

"Easy," said Tokta. "Any young person of any age may

enter, and they must gather tomorrow morning in front of that farthest yurt. Haza will be there. He will announce the directions, and when the horn sounds, you must ride like all the spirits of all the demons in these mountains are chasing you! Clearly, whoever returns first, wins."

"I'm watching the other riders to check on my competition," Chengli said. But I'm watching, he thought, and I'm making a plan. White Beard will be proud.

At dinner that night, he sat with the cousins on the grass in front of the yurt.

"Hojanias," Chengli said, "some riders have eagle feathers stuck in the top of their hats. Long ago I asked Agha about them. He said they were for luck. I need luck." He looked at Tokta. "I need a lot of luck! How can I get feathers for my hat?" He pulled off his hat and punched at the top.

Tokta's mouth dropped open. "Luck?" he gasped, and threw up his hands in pretended horror. "It's more than luck, Little Brother. *You* will never have eagle feathers. They announce to the world that the brave wearer has stolen a horse!"

At sunrise the next morning, Chengli awoke and pounced upon Hojanias and Tokta. "Wake up! Today's the day!" He opened the tent flap and looked out into the sunlight. "The race. The contest. The win-or-be-eaten-alive day! I'm ready. Let's go!"

"This race will be a test of everything I've taught you, Little Brother," said Hojanias as he joined Chengli. "It is rough and brutal and long, very long—all day long. The main thing is . . . stay on your horse!"

"I know," Chengli answered. "It's more skill than speed, and you've taught me well. We'll go down the valley, over the mountain, along the ridge, into the next valley, and around the tents with orange flags flying. Then home." He laughed a short, nervous laugh.

They left the tent and made their way to the crowd gathering in the field. Women laid blankets on the ground to claim their space. Men worked with their sons and daughters to secure the horses. Across the valley, anyone who had no work to do reveled in the warmth of early spring. Men sat in circles thumping frantically on their drums, while women and children stamped and whirled to the rhythm.

Chengli saddled his horse and checked the lashings. Hojanias stood beside him and warned, "Better tie everything twice. Things can get rough."

"I have no way to thank you for the weeks and months you've helped me," Chengli said, leaning down to speak quietly to Hojanias. "If I'm successful today, I won't win the race at all, but I'll win my own prize. If my plan works, I can't come back to thank you. And if I fail . . ."

Hojanias stopped him. "Go, Little Brother. Race your best! We will cheer for you and remember you always. Go."

Chengli turned and rode into the tangled mass of horses and riders. The race, he knew, had only one rule: do not start until . . .

The horn sounded!

A hundred horses bolted forward. Chengli hung on as his horse galloped, trapped in the crush of horseflesh and screaming children. "Great spirit of my long-dead-horse-riding-honorable-father," he yelled into the chaos, "make me a son worthy of my father! Keep me on my horse!"

They hurtled forward across the valley.

Chengli's thoughts dissolved into noise.

Pushing.

Shoving.

Pounding.

Past the tents, up into the mountain.

Minutes came and went. Hours came and went. Trees, branches, rocks, and streams blurred and swayed and blurred again.

Horses struggled, reared, bucked, and snorted. Chengli slipped sideways, grabbed his horse's mane, and heard Hojanias's words, "Stay on your horse!"

A boy fell. No one stopped to see if he was hurt. The sun glared. Dust blinded. Sweat poured. Hooves pounded. The riders thundered along the ridge and headed down into the last valley. Sweat rolled into Chengli's eyes. He reached down to rub his face on his sleeve and jabbed his wrist against his nose instead. It bled. He ignored it.

Up ahead, above the bobbing, swaying mass of riders, he glimpsed the orange flags. Halfway. He'd made it halfway.

His thoughts cleared. Behind him he could hear the pounding of hooves and the yelling of riders, so he wasn't at the end of the pack. He'd managed to stay in the middle. Not bad! Not bad at all.

"Turn, turn! Don't fall off!" Chengli yelled loudly at himself. He couldn't hear a word over the din. "Hang on!" he yelled again.

With muscles sore and vision blurred, he realized he had reached the mountain leading back down to Haza's valley. "Now!" he called out. "The plan!"

Charging full speed down the steep slope, dodging trees and boulders, Chengli gradually forced his horse out to the edge of the pack. When the sea of riders flowed around a bend to the left, Chengli pulled with all his might and forced his horse to the right, crashing into the prickly branches of the trees and sending a shower of cones to the ground.

He worked to calm the horse. He rubbed and talked, talked and rubbed, and slowly brought the horse to a panting, trembling stop. Leaning down, he rested his exhausted head on the horse's neck. "Thank you, spirit of my honorable father," he mumbled and grinned. "I stayed on my horse!"

He raised his head and looked out between the trees. Good, he thought, no one noticed me leave.

He worked his way along the mountainside, staying deep behind the curtain of trees. When he caught a glimpse of the tents and careening riders below, he got off the horse. No one must see him. Or hear him. He moved slowly until he saw that he was above the outer edge of Haza's camp, above the stream. He found a shelter for the horse between two boulders and tied the horse to a tree. Then slowly he moved down the mountain, staying in the shadow of the trees, until he reached a spot directly above the stream. He sat down to wait.

Sooner or later, he knew, Meiling must come there for water.

The sun dropped behind the trees. Shadows lengthened. Sweat dried on Chengli's back and made him shiver. He sat bunched up in a ball and tried not to shake. He had to be ready.

Across the stream, carried upon the evening air, came the shouts of victory, the thumping of the drums, and the pounding and clapping of the dancers. Everyone celebrated the race—children, grownups, winner, survivors. He knew that anyone who remembered him would simply think he was somewhere in the crowd. He waited.

The sound of splashing water caught his attention. There they were: the girls in brown. Please, oh please take your time, he silently begged.

The girls filled their buckets and turned away. Chengli winced. No, no, no! He wet his lips and tried to whistle. No sound. He tried again. A soft whistle, a soft bird call.

Meiling stiffened. She lost her balance, and the water bucket tumbled to the ground. "Oh no! Go ahead," she called to her companion. "I've got to go back for more water."

Chengli watched from behind the tree. When Meiling reached the stream, she turned slightly as she bent to fill the bucket. "Are you there?" she whispered.

"Hurry," Chengli answered. "Over here!" He reached out one hand to direct her.

Meiling put down her bucket and inched her way across the stream. Without a word, she grabbed Chengli's hand and ducked down behind the protecting tree.

"No, no, don't stop," he whispered. "I've got a horse tied up above."

They scrambled up the hillside, moving silently from tree to tree. A shadow loomed in front of them.
Chengli yanked at Meiling's arm and pulled her aside.

Too late. A crack on the head sent him plunging to the ground.

fifteen

CHENGLI AWOKE IN THE GLOOM AND SILENCE OF A TENT. He rubbed his wrists and found they were not bound. He turned his head to look across the tent. A mistake. Pain shot down his neck and across his shoulders. He groaned and lay still, praying to the mountain spirits for help.

"Wake up," came a voice. "Wake up!"

He forced open his eyes, and Meiling's face came into focus.

"Shhhh," she whispered. "Haza's men found us. They are outside."

"Where are we?" Chengli whispered back. "Why aren't we tied up?"

"They don't have to tie us," she said. "They are clever. This tent has camel bells sewn all along the bottom edge, so if anyone lifts the tent wall, the bells will sound and alert the guards."

"Is there a guard?" Chengli asked.

"Of course. Two of them. Sitting right outside the door flap."

Chengli closed his eyes and rubbed his aching head. What now, old White Beard? What do I do now? He ran his hands through his short-cropped hair and rolled his shoulders to rid them of their stiffness. Failed, failed, failed again—the words ran around and around in his head.

In disgust, he lay back on the carpet. He opened his eyes and looked without seeing. A circle of light shone into his eyes. He squinted. The light made his head hurt.

Light? The smoke hole. His vision cleared and he stared at the opening. He signaled to get Meiling's attention and then nodded upward.

"The smoke hole. We will get out through that!" he whispered. "Come on."

"Impossible!" Meiling mouthed without a sound.

"No, really. We can't move the cloth at the bottom of the tent, you're right. That would shake the tent and make the bells sound. But the tent is made with layers of strong felt. Once we are outside, we can grab hold of the felt and lower ourselves slowly down the outside, hand over hand. I'll go first, and then I can help you. We can climb to the smoke hole if we stand on that," and he pointed to a small table.

"Wait! Let me check on the guards." Meiling peeked through the crack where the door flap let in light. "They are not thinking of us at all. They are watching the horses get ready for the Dispute of the Sheep." She moved back into the center of the tent. "I'm sure they'd rather be riding in the game than sitting there on the stones. The field is cluttered with horses!"

"Listen to the yelling and shouting out there!" Chengli sat up.

"And the horses neighing and hooves pounding. The game must be starting." She peeped out again. "Yes! The guards are standing, trying to see the action!"

"Perfect for us," Chengli said. "Hurry." He pulled a low table to the center of the tent under the smoke hole. Meiling dragged over a thick cushion, and together they shoved it onto the table.

Chengli climbed up. It wasn't high enough, so they added another cushion. He tried again and was able to touch the circle of wood that supported the opening.

"It may work," he said softly. "Even if the guards turn around, they won't think to look *up*. I'll hoist myself up— you help by pushing up on my feet—that's it." He stopped. "Wait. I've got to get something." He eased himself down, went over to the wall where a hat hung on a peg. Reaching up, he yanked three eagle feathers from the top of the hat and stuck them under his belt.

"What are those for?" asked Meiling.

Chengli's only answer was a grin as he climbed back onto the cushions and reached again toward the smoke hole.

Gradually his head, then his arms, poked out of the hole. Meiling shoved from below, and carefully, silently, he pulled himself out and lay stretched on the back side of the round tent top.

"Your turn! Stretch up," he whispered. "You can do it." He reached down into the hole until he felt Meiling's hands. He pulled until she could grasp the wooden ring of the smoke hole. Then he caught her under her arms and pulled until her head and shoulders wiggled out.

She rolled inch by inch out onto the tent top, pulled out

her feet, and began the silent task of lowering herself to the ground. She balanced on one and then another of the ropes that lashed the felt tent sides into place. Chengli followed.

When he reached the ground, he stood still, listening, thinking. Now what?

He imagined White Beard standing there with them, and he talked to the old grandfather in his head. He had learned one thing. He could plan. And plans didn't have to be made in advance. You could make up plans *quickly*. And a good plan—Chengli glanced around—a good plan was when you tried to think of what would happen next.

From here he could go straight across the stream and up the mountain to the horse. But what happened next would be that someone would see them and capture them again.

He looked to his left, along the back of the remaining yurts and away from the commotion of the galloping horses. All he saw were some meandering sheep and a few clothes hung over a bush to dry. The clothes looked like women's clothes, embroidered in bright red, blue, and yellow. The sheep munched grass just beyond the clothes.

"That's it! Come on," Chengli whispered. "I'm used to sheep from my life with Hojanias, so just walk slowly as if we are caring for the sheep and don't look back."

He led Meiling to the bushes behind the tents and lifted off two skirts from the bush. Her puzzled look disappeared. She grinned and pulled down a jacket, vest, and two head scarves.

Hugging their treasures, they moved behind the last yurt and put their new clothes on right over the old. The long skirts had to be fastened up under their arms, but the strange fit was covered by the jacket and vest. Meiling giggled.

"Here we go. Two girls taking their sheep to higher pasture." Chengli pointed down the valley, away from the crowds, and also away from the path to their horse. He picked up a stick and prodded the sheep into line.

"Move gently. Move slowly," he cautioned quietly.

They moved down the valley, following the sheep, until they saw an open space high on the hill along the edge of the forest.

"There's a good place to take sheep. When we get up there, we can leave the sheep and duck into the forest." Chengli drove the sheep across the stream and up the hill. The hill was steep. The sheep were slow. Chengli glanced back and saw people gathered near the bushes.

"Wondering what happened to their clothes," he said.

Meiling looked back. "They're pointing up here!" she breathed. "They know who we are!"

"Run!" shouted Chengli. "They're sending a dog!"

The yapping of the dog grew louder as it bounded up the hill.

"Over here," Chengli yelled. "The path bends out of their view. Get behind me! I'll take care of the dog!"

He grabbed a fallen tree branch and turned to face the attacking dog. Barking ferociously, it leaped at Meiling and bit into her arm.

"Aiii!" Meiling screamed as blood spurted from the wound. The dog jumped up for another attack, but Chengli lunged at it with all his strength. The tree branch made contact. The dog whimpered and lay still.

"I'm dying! I'm dying!" sobbed Meiling as she dropped to the ground. "And you've killed the dog!"

"You're not dying and neither is the dog," grunted Chengli. "It's just stunned and already waking up." He grabbed at the scarf tied around his head and yanked it down over the dog's feet. "This will hold him still," gasped Chengli. "It's the hobble I use on our camels!" He pulled the scarf in two loops around the dog's forelegs and forced them close together. Another loop yanked the left hind leg tight against the other two. He quickly knotted the three legs together and jumped out of reach as the dog woke up. It snapped and snarled but could only thrash around helplessly on the ground.

Chengli pulled Meiling toward the trees. "That dog bit right through your arm," Chengli said. "Give me your head scarf. I'll wrap it around the wound as tight as I can. That should stop the bleeding. We'll have to clean it, but we can't stop now. We'll clean it at the first stream we find."

As Chengli worked, Meiling groaned, clutched at her arm, and fought back the tears.

"We've got to get out of here," Chengli said, looking back. "I can't see anybody. That means they can't see us. Here, drop the vest and your stolen skirt. I'll do the same. When they get here, they will be sure that we dropped the clothes as we ran this way."

"Well, it's true," gasped Meiling.

"No, not at all," Chengli said. He helped Meiling to her feet and turned so that he could hoist her up onto his back. Stumbling under Meiling's weight, he crossed the grass and moved into the forest, heading back toward the settlement.

"What are you doing?" Meiling whispered. "We can't go back!"

"That is exactly what Haza and his men will think," said Chengli. "But we are high above the valley now. No one will think to look this way. Shhh. I hear them."

Chengli stopped and set Meiling down under the branches of a spruce tree. In the distance they saw two of Haza's men rounding the bend right where the clothes were dumped. The man in front saw the jacket and waved to his companion. The two men disappeared, following the trail that Chengli had set.

"Come on, now we can move. We must stay hidden, but there is no need to hurry. The men have gone the other way." He looked at Meiling, her face white with pain. Please don't die, he thought. I've spent months trying to find you. Don't die now.

Chengli carried the princess on his back until they reached the boulders where he had hidden his horse. What if the horse wasn't there? What if someone had found it and waited there to capture them again? What if . . .

"We're here," he said to Meiling as he turned the corner into the enclosure, "and we are safe! The horse is here, just the way I left it."

He set Meiling on the ground and threw himself down full length beside her as she lay sobbing and laughing.

"I'm all mixed up," said Meiling between sobs. "I'm happy and scared and tired and my arm hurts. It really hurts."

"I wish we could rest, but we have to get away from here." Chengli helped Meiling get on the horse, then he walked in front, leading. Up through the trees they picked their way until they crossed over the ridge.

"Now," said Chengli, "we can ride. No, wait!"

He took his hat from where it was tucked under the saddle blanket, pulled the crumpled eagle feathers out from under his belt, and jabbed them into the top of his hat.

"Hojanias! Tokta!" he called into the wind. "See my eagle feathers? They tell the world that I am now an official thief! I am rescuing the princess, but to do it, I am stealing your horse!"

sixteen

THE NEXT FEW DAYS TWISTED THEMSELVES INTO A KNOT OF JOY AND TERROR, and the knot sat in the pit of Chengli's stomach.

He first rode in joy because he was free—and he had his princess. But terror pushed away the joy because she was dying right in front of his eyes, and there was nothing he could do to help her. Her arm burned red and angry. The wound reeked with ugly green slime, and fever racked her body. Sometimes she knew who he was, but mostly she lay slumped across the horse's neck, and Chengli hung on to her so she wouldn't fall off.

Thoughts in his head changed with the rhythm of the horse's progress down the mountain. He knew that Master Fong's caravan should still be in Kashgar. They would be watching the high western mountains, waiting for the snow to melt and the trail to open. Chengli knew he could reach Kashgar if he kept going with the sun coming up on his left and going down on his right.

"Meiling," he said as he tried to keep her awake on the ride, "Meiling, I know I should call you Princess, but I've stopped thinking of you as Princess. You used to be so awful. Do you remember those days?" He chuckled, recalling her demanding voice. She made no sign of hearing him. He wondered if she heard anything in her feverish state.

They rode along with nothing in sight but endless ridges and stretches of forest that gradually gave way to slopes as barren and brown as the desert below. Chengli talked, hoping she could hear. "I started out to rescue you because I felt guilty. It was my fault you got kidnapped. But somewhere over the winter, I came to think of you as a friend—a friend who absolutely must not be sold as a slave. Now I've found you. Please, oh please," he murmured as he rubbed her back and pushed the damp hair from her face, "please don't die."

As the wish escaped his lips, he stopped the horse. They stood on top of the final ridge; far below rolled the familiar brown of the desert. Down there somewhere lay the huge caravan center of Kashgar.

Kashgar reigned as the fabled city where all caravan routes from all the mountains and deserts—east, west, south, and north—came together. Kashgar, hemmed in on three sides by mountains that reached into the clouds and on the fourth side by the endless shifting sands of the Taklamakan Desert.

Chengli looked across the distance at the white snow peaks that ringed the desert as far as he could see and blocked all caravan travel. When that snow began to melt, caravans could move again along the trails. But spring had yet to come to the high mountains, and the white line of snow hovered just above the city. The caravans waited. Master Fong's group must be somewhere in the crowd.

By evening the exhausted horse and riders had reached the first caravan field.

"Master Fong! Master Fong!" Chengli called out, right and left. No one answered.

He'd forgotten the stink of a field packed solid with camels and donkeys. He gagged but kept moving and calling out. He fought to hold Meiling steady. He called out again.

"Master Fong! Uncle Tao! Abdul! Bori! Are you here?"

"Here, over here," came a reply at last. "Who seeks Master Fong's caravan?"

Chengli guided the horse toward the voice. "Help us. Oh please, help us!" He stopped the horse and whispered, "I am Chengli, the one who disappeared at Kucha. I have the girl, but she is dying. Maybe she is dead."

He felt strong arms pulling Meiling out of his grasp. More arms lifted him out of the saddle. He was asleep before his feet touched the ground.

He slept until someone shook him, and daylight warmed his face. Uncle Tao—dear, friendly, rough, and wrinkled Uncle Tao, his hair still black, his beard still white—sat beside him, filling the tent with the comforting smell of a familiar friend.

"I have tended the little slave girl," he said. "Her arm is damaged, but she lives. I have washed the wound with freshly boiled water and dressed it with ointment. Now we must wait." He sighed. "We have little else to do here but wait. We wait for news of our master."

"Is it true he has vanished?" Chengli asked.

"True indeed. The nomad king came to claim his bride, and we had no bride to give him. Master Fong did not want to die—so he disappeared instead!"

Chengli sat up. "Uncle Tao, where can he be? He can come back now. The slave girl you are nursing is our princess! I found her. She's here now. Master Fong will be safe."

A rough voice broke apart their conversation. "Here he is! Arrest him!"

Fourth Brother, with the same sneer on his face and anger in his voice, pushed past Uncle Tao, grabbed Chengli by the shoulder, and pulled him to his feet. Behind Fourth Brother came two rough policemen, their long tridents announcing their authority.

"He crept in last night in the dark," Fourth Brother said to the police, "hoping I wouldn't notice. He's the one you want. I *saw* him ride off from Kucha with a stolen horse and the imperial princess! Arrest him!"

"That's not true!" Chengli coughed in his exhaustion, but the men held him fast. He glanced in disbelief at Fourth Brother, and then whispered to Uncle Tao, "Take care of the girl! I'll be right back!"

But he didn't come back. Instead, he sat huddled against the wall of a dark, damp cell and tried to figure out where things had gone wrong. He got up and banged his fists against the door of his cell, yelled out his innocence. No one came. No one listened. He sat alone in the nearly complete darkness of a dirt cell.

Footsteps sounded in the outer corridor. They stopped outside his cell door.

"Get up, boy," a voice ordered. "The magistrate, Judge Yen, will see you now."

The guard yanked open the cell door, pulled Chengli to his feet, and walked him down a narrow passageway and out across a courtyard. Sunlight glared against his face. He walked with his head down and his eyes nearly closed against the bright light of the sun. This was not the way the son of Inspector Chao should be meeting the magistrate, the man who held the power of life and death in his decisions.

"Boy," the magistrate, Judge Yen, said when Chengli knelt before him, "you are charged with a terrible crime. Another has accused you. You must hear what he has said and verify the accuracy of the writing by putting your thumbprint on this document board." The judge picked up a paper and slowly read the accusation. Chengli noticed that his voice, although severe, was not unkind. It gave him hope.

Chengli listened carefully to the report, even though he knew already what Fourth Brother had said.

"Most Honorable Judge, may I speak?"

"Speak," the judge answered.

"That report is not accurate," Chengli said softly, keeping his head down, talking into the floor. "I cannot sign." He cleared his throat and tried again. "I did not steal the princess. Bandits kidnapped her. I chased after her and searched for her for months all across the high mountains. With the Kazakhs' help, I found her and rescued her. But," he continued, "there is no one here to tell you my story is true. If the princess lives, she will tell you. But she is dying. She is with Master Fong's caravan."

"There is no one else who can speak for you?" asked the magistrate.

"No one. My father, Inspector Chao, would speak for me, but he has left this world for the world of our ancestors." Chengli felt at the pouch that carried the piece of jade.

The judge's eyes grew round with astonishment. "What is this mention of Inspector Chao?" he asked.

"He is my father," answered Chengli.

"You lie!" thundered the judge. "You come here a filthy, ragged slave, a camel driver, and expect me to believe you were born to one of our most learned and wise inspectors? Your crime is compounded by your arrogance! Return to your cell!"

"Please, Your Excellency," begged Chengli. "I lost my father to bandits and my mother to illness. I grew up in the silk merchant's business in Chang'an. It was my choice to come back to the desert and learn of my father . . . and that's all true." Chengli sank exhausted to the floor and waited.

"You expect me to believe all that?" asked the judge. "Just because you share the same family name of Chao does not prove you are his son."

Chengli rubbed the jade at his side, remembering the coolness it had given him the first time he held it, and decided he must take a chance. "I have only this piece of broken jade that I am told once belonged to my father." He took out the talisman and handed it to the judge. "I do not know if it's important, but it is all I have."

The judge inhaled and then whispered, "I know that jade!"

Chengli stiffened with surprise and waited.

"There is more to this story than one piece of broken jade," continued the judge, "but since you kneel here before me awaiting a trial of life or death, I will keep silent until we work through the trial. If you live, we will speak more of this matter. If you die, you will not care about one piece of broken jade."

Judge Yen stood and drew in a long, slow breath. "To prepare for a life-and-death trial, I must spend three days reviewing the case—without eating meat or listening to music. I must consider my thoughts and the wisdom of the heavens. I must listen to the spirits for guidance." He moved toward the door. "In the meantime," he added, "you may keep the jade."

The guards marched Chengli back to his cell.

✝ た
seventeen

Outside, the wind whistled and moaned. It rattled against the outer wall of the jail like a living thing. With his eyes closed, Chengli sat on the dirt floor of his cell and listened to it wail. *You pulled me into the desert, old demon wind, and now you've pushed me into jail. What do you want?* he wondered.

He reached into the pouch at his side and felt the jade. *Maybe,* he thought, *I'll never find the other half of this. Maybe Father took it with him into the spirit world.* In the darkness, Chengli smelled the fragrant breeze of the mountain meadow, and in the meadow he saw White Beard. The old grandfather had often talked of the Kazakhs' trained eagles, and how, when the birds got too old or tired to hunt, their owners set them free. Could it be that when the bandits took his father's life, they had set his spirit free?

Thinking such thoughts, he sat and waited.

When the trial came, it came swiftly. The tribunal had been prepared for the trial, with torches lit by the main gate, announcing to all that a life-and-death decision was about to begin. Citizens filed into the room and stood in respectful silence. Guards walked Chengli into the courtroom and shoved him to his knees in front of the raised platform. Around the room and out in the open yard, he saw the crowd of townspeople who had come to listen. They stood, eagerly waiting to criticize or cheer the decision of the judge. In the front row stood—he blinked—Master Fong! Chengli jumped up; the guard shoved him back down, nearly cracking his skull on the hard floor. Chengli grinned in spite of his pain—Master had left the safety of his hiding place and come to attend the trial. Chengli felt stronger and more hopeful just at the sight of him.

The judge entered, clad in his full ceremonial robe of shimmering blue silk, with a black gauze cap covering his hair. He sat behind a high bench on the raised platform and looked around the crowded hall. He spoke to the crowd. "My job," he said, "is to establish the facts and hand out punishment. Fourth Brother, here on the right, has accused the boy on my left—family name of Chao, personal name of Chengli—of stealing imperial property, namely, a royal princess. Chao Chengli tells me that he, instead, rescued this very princess."

The judge cleared his throat and continued. "It is one person's word against the other, and neither can produce a witness to speak on their behalf. The punishment for tampering with imperial property," he stopped and looked at Chengli, "is death by hanging."

The crowd inhaled as one. Murmurs shivered around the room like the buzz of many mosquitoes. Chengli gasped for breath to keep from fainting.

Suddenly a voice cut through the mumbling like the slash of a sword—a voice Chengli recognized. "The judge!" called the voice. "We've come to see the judge!" And from the back of the room came Uncle Tao, striding directly up to the judge without a quiver of fear in his body. In his arms he carried the princess.

"Silence and order!" Judge Yen hit the gavel hard on the table.

"We cannot be silent! Please, O Honorable One, I bring a witness," Uncle Tao called out.

The crowd murmured as they watched Uncle Tao, who moved to the front and waited for the judge to address him.

"He brings a witness!" whispered a woman's voice.

"Let the witness be heard," called out a man's voice.

The judge nodded his head. "Who is this?" he asked Uncle Tao.

"She is the very Royal Princess Meiling, around whom this case revolves," answered Uncle Tao. "She alone can tell you what really happened."

Uncle Tao carried Meiling forward and held her up to the judge. In a soft, barely audible voice, she told her story to the judge, and the judge repeated it to the crowd. While she spoke, everyone looked back and forth from Chengli to Fourth Brother. There was total silence so that her words would not be lost. Uncle Tao returned to his place and set Meiling down.

Finally the judge spoke. "This is indeed a sad case, and it grows more so. Our law dictates that if one person accuses another, and that accusation is found to be false," he stopped and looked directly at Fourth Brother, "the two must change places. The accused must go free, and the false accuser must suffer the planned punishment."

Uncle Tao looked quickly from Fourth Brother to the judge. "But Your Eminence," he whispered, "the boy is young. Is there not some other answer?"

The judge sat silently behind his lacquered table, tugging thoughtfully at his beard. He looked at the crowd. He looked at Chengli. He looked down at his own hands, turning them over and back as if they held some special message. Then he spoke.

"In deciding a case of life or death, I must think carefully. I must use my own knowledge, and I must use knowledge that comes to me from the spirits. It is important that the affairs of earth be in harmony with the will of heaven."

The people murmured approval.

The judge stood up. "As magistrate, I base my decision on the words of the princess and," he nodded to the crowd, "on the advice of the spirits."

The people grinned.

"Death is too strong for a young man with potential," said the judge, "but his crime of lying nearly destroyed an innocent human being. Here is my decision."

The crowd waited.

"Chao Chengli, you may go free."

The crowd buzzed with approval.

"Fourth Brother, I give you two orders. One, you will stay with the caravan and return to the Middle Kingdom. Two, you will take charge of all finances for the caravan and be responsible for all sales. They will be correct." The judge called Master Fong to come forward. "Master Fong, this young man must serve you faithfully as long as he lives."

The crowd of villagers grew restless at this turn of events. "The liar deserves his punishment!" they called out. "He was willing to destroy the younger boy," said another. "He deserves to die!" But the judge held up his hand and silenced them.

Master Fong shook his head in confusion. "Fourth Brother is a good worker, and he knows his job. He is worth saving. But," Master Fong twisted his hands nervously, "how can I trust him after what he has done?"

"Because," the judge said, "I now speak to him. Fourth Brother, come before me."

Fourth Brother knelt in front of the judge's lacquered table and knocked his head solidly on the floor several times. Chengli saw how he trembled.

"Listen carefully," said the judge. "You have no choice if you wish to stay alive: Be faithful. Learn the finances of the caravan and keep strict order. Fail—and be hanged."

The people stood in stunned silence as the announcement sank in. Then slowly, the crowd of onlookers made room as Uncle Tao went forward to retrieve Fourth Brother. Master Fong, moving to the side of Chengli, stopped at the sound of the magistrate's voice.

"Master Fong and Chao Chengli, follow me to my private room."

Glancing at each other in confusion, Chengli and his master obeyed.

Once behind the closed door, the judge motioned them both up from kneeling and pointed them to chairs. "The terror of this trial is now over," he said. "The princess has provided the rightful ending, and your spirits may be in peace. Do not tremble," he said, glancing at the worried expressions of both waiting faces. "I have something of interest to tell Chengli, and I think you, Master Fong, should be aware of it as well."

Chengli waited, wondering what would follow.

he judge continued. "This boy has shown me a piece of broken jade, left to him by his father. I know the full story of this jade. Inspector Chao had made several trips to the southern oasis of Khotan, famous for its valuable jade of fresh greens and whites, and he collected a number of lovely pieces. All are valuable—some are worth an entire year's salary. One day he came to me saying that he had been ordered to move against a band of smugglers, and he feared for his life. He handed me his box of jade pieces, asking that it be returned to him if he succeeded, or given to his wife and infant son if he failed. When I asked him how I would recognize his wife or son, he broke a piece in half. 'Here,' he said, 'I will give half to you and half to my wife . . . with it, she can claim the rest.' " The judge stopped and watched Chengli.

"So what Old Cook told is true," said Chengli in wonder. "Mother knew she was dying, gave the broken jade to the cook, and Old Cook gave it to me. But, now, if you give it to me, what will I do with it? I don't really want it. I can't keep it safe on the caravan, and I don't know what to do with it!" Chengli looked imploringly at the judge.

"Can you read and write?" asked the judge.

"No, Your Honor. I've always been a servant or a camel driver. Such learning is not for servants."

"Ah," said the judge, "but as you say, you are Inspector Chao's son. To become an inspector, your father learned the thousands of Chinese writing characters and studied the writings of the ancient wise teacher Confucius. With that knowledge, he took and passed the government exam and rose to the rank of inspector. Had he lived, surely he would have risen higher." The judge paused, watching Chengli. "And had he lived, his son would have had a teacher, to learn and to rise, as did his father."

"But I am too old to begin learning," said Chengli, "and there is no need for a scholar on the caravan." This thought of learning from books had never entered Chengli's mind. He wasn't at all sure that he'd like to spend all day inside studying.

"Indeed, since you first appeared before me, I've been pondering that," said the judge, "and that is why I asked Master Fong to join us. I suggest—and I think your father would have agreed—that the jade be used to pay for your schooling. Master Fong, if you are willing, I will give the box of jade into your safekeeping." The judge took from his drawer a box, opened it, and spread the pieces of pale green and white jade across the table.

"You, Chengli," the judge continued, "will stay with the caravan until it returns again to Chang'an, the home of many great scholars and teachers. Once there, your master will use his knowledge of the local people to locate a scholar who agrees both to provide you with room and board and mentor you until you pass the government exam. The jade will be used to pay your teacher."

Chengli gasped. He didn't think he wanted to do what the judge suggested, for learning to read and write meant learning many thousands of complicated written characters before he could even begin to study the books of the great teacher Confucius on which the entire exam was based. But Master Fong looked delighted.

The judge returned the jade pieces to their box. He handed the box to Master Fong and turned again to Chengli. "The idea of learning is new to you and worries you—I can tell by your face—but think about it. You have many months before you get back to Chang'an, and by then you may come to like the idea. Certainly the spirit of your father will be delighted!" The judge chuckled at the thought.

"Now," he continued, "let me tell you more about the broken piece. Your piece has on it the word 'breeze.' My half, the one that completes the circle, says 'mountain.' I recall that Inspector Chao once told me that if he held the jade disk in his hand, the winds of the hot desert became as refreshing as a soft mountain breeze. I myself never felt it." With that, he waved his hand to dismiss them both, but stopped.

"Chao Chengli," said the judge, "you are indeed your father's son. At your young age, you have already demonstrated his honesty and his courage. So when you have succeeded and passed the government exam, as I know you will, come back here to Kashgar. I will want to congratulate you—and perhaps even help you get a good position!"

For the next few days, everyone hovered close to Master Fong's caravan and worked at recovering from the trial. Fourth Brother stayed out of sight. Chengli began again his care of the animals and didn't have time to fret about the jade and the responsibility it brought. Meiling spent more and more time remembering how to be a princess. From her cart, she took the royal dresses and hung them out to air in the sunlight. When the work was done, she went to join Chengli, putting out the food for the donkeys.

"What will you do now?" she asked him.

"Emmmm?" he looked up, his voice a question.

"I've changed, you know," she continued, picking up the shovel and jabbing it into the ground. "I learned one thing in the mountains. It will be better to be the bride of a nomad king than the slave of a bandit! I am ready for the arrival of King Galdan." She thought a minute and then added, "I have decided: you will go with me."

"What?" Chengli jumped up and stared at her.

"Yes," she said. "You shall go with me into my new life. I have no one left from my old life except Sudarshana, Dakshesh, and you, Camel Boy. You risked your life to rescue me. Come with me. You are more than my servant . . . you are my friend . . . no," she smiled, "you are my elder brother!"

"Yes," Chengli said, grinning. "I will serve you faithfully!" He stopped. The grin left his face. "No, it is not possible, Princess. A camel boy cannot be brother to a princess, and," he hesitated, "the judge has told me to return to Chang'an to commence my studies."

Meiling stared at him in surprise. She pulled herself up taller and straighter. The sister became the princess. She glared at Chengli.

Chengli leaned back against the warm body of the donkey. He shook his head as if to clear confusion. "No, Princess. You will have many servants in your new life. Master Fong has been good to me."

He hesitated. A new thought suddenly took hold: My spirit father helped me find Meiling. He helped me ride like a Kazakh. But the caravan master has become a real father to me!

Out loud he said only, "The caravan needs good workers, and I am good with the camels. It will take the caravan many months to return to Chang'an, and until we reach the imperial city again, I will work for Master Fong."

The days grew warm. Men bartered, traded, and packed for their next journey. Some planned to trade their camels for horses and go west over the cloud-touching mountains. Master Fong planned to sell his loads to those continuing west, purchase new treasures from the distant western caravans, and turn back across the desert to return to Chang'an.

In the midst of their work, a messenger came to announce that King Galdan would arrive the following day to claim his bride. He would await them at the northern edge of the caravan field.

Everyone helped Meiling get ready. They swept out the cart, packed her few belongings, and, when the morning dawned, dressed in their finest clothes and went out to meet the king.

Chengli kept to the back and watched the little parade. First walked Master Fong and Uncle Tao, both dressed in their finest robes. Then came Meiling riding Hojanias's horse. Behind her walked her guards and her new cook.

Ahead of them, at the edge of the field, waited a line of horse riders—rough men with swords at their sides. As Master brought his little group to a halt, an old man rode forward through the protective line of guards.

Oh no, thought Chengli, the king is old!

Meiling glanced up and saw the old man. Her face drained of all its color, but she did not move.

"She looks every bit the royal princess," said Chengli to himself.

The man spoke. "I am the messenger for our Honorable King Galdan, who welcomes you as his bride." He reached up, took the reins of Meiling's horse, and began to guide her through the tunnel of guards toward a young man sitting tall on his powerful horse. His heavily bearded face and his clothes of felt and fur skins marked him as a nomad. Meiling relaxed when she saw his friendly smile, and the color returned to her cheeks.

"Wait!" called out Chengli, bolting forward past his master and Uncle Tao.

The nomad guards swung around and raised their swords to protect their princess. Chengli dropped to the ground smashing his forehead into the dirt. He cringed, braced for the slash of the swords against his neck.

"No! Lower your swords!" Meiling's voice rang out, hard with authority. To Dakshesh she said, "Go and see what the camel boy wants."

The old man held Meiling's horse and waited. Chengli picked himself up out of the dirt and slowly walked forward, facing the ground. When he reached Dakshesh, he held out his broken piece of jade.

"Take this to the princess," he said, his voice barely a whisper. "I cannot go with her into her new life. Instead I offer her the only thing of value that is mine to give. Take my jade to her." He held out the two pieces of jade. The green color shimmered in the sunlight. The princess watched the proceeding but did not move. He tried again. "Please, take it to her. And tell her when she holds it to remember her caravan boy."

He held it out again.

Meiling looked steadily at Chengli, and her eyes filled with tears. Wiping her eyes with the corner of her silk sleeve, she motioned Dakshesh to her side. She leaned over and took the jade, slowly closing her fingers around the twice-precious stone.

Then with a nod to Chengli, the old man turned and led Meiling to the waiting king.

Chengli stood with a pain stabbing his stomach and watched the princess and her new family ride away. A wind, yellow with desert dust, rolled and danced around their feet. A demon wind, it rose and hid the princess from his view. A spirit wind, it stung his eyes and blew against his heart.

Master Fong and Uncle Tao stood beside him, one on each side. Together they turned and walked back to the caravan.

Historical Notes
Where Imagination Meets Reality

ALL PLACES ARE REAL; ALL PEOPLE ARE IMAGINED.

Except for Chang'an, all Chinese cities and towns are given their modern name so that readers can find them on a map. The ancient name is noted if it is different from the current one.

Camels: There are two kinds of camels. The one-hump Arabian camel (dromedary) lives mainly in Africa and Arabia. The Bactrian camel (with two humps) lives in Asia.

Chang'an (the current Xian): Imperial city of the Tang Dynasty (618-907 CE) with eastern and western markets, bell tower, and drum tower that sounded to open and close the city gates.

Dunhuang: Hundreds of Buddhist cave temples were carved into the cliffs, of which the Mogao Caves are the most famous. Crescent Lake still exists and the sand dune festival was an ancient custom even at the time of this story.

Hami melons: Hami melons, then and now, are sold all over China and have recently shown up in American markets. (The ancient name for the town of Hami was Yiwu).

Kashgar: For thousands of years Kashgar has been and still is a caravan and trade center at the crossroads of north-south and east-west routes.

Kazakh music: Music has always been closely intertwined with Kazakh nomadic life, and everyday life was accompanied by song. Traveling storyteller-musicians called *akyn* are still an important part of Kazakh life, and spontaneous contests demand quick musical answers to sudden jokes and questions.

Khotan (ancient city's name was Yutian): Famous both then and now for excellent jade of various colors.

Kucha: Famous for its music, which influenced all Chinese music. Thousands of musicians and dancers from Kucha performed in the imperial court in Chang'an.

Law: The law used at the trial is called "wu gao fan zuo," which means "wrong accusation punishment returns." It is more ancient than this story, and it existed before the Tang Dynasty (618-907 CE)

Mountains: The desert in this story is surrounded on three sides by some of the highest mountains in the world, causing difficulties for any travelers attempting to cross over them. Think of the letter "U" lying on its side with the open end facing east. Along the north run the Tian Shan (Heavenly Mountains), named perhaps for their height (reaching 25,000 feet) or for the spruce forests on their lower slopes. The west is blocked by the Pamir mountains, a treeless expanse of rock. To the south come the Hindu Kush, where "kush" means death and perhaps reflects the dangers in crossing over these barren, rocky, and landslide-prone mountains. Finally come the Kunlun chain, with their highest peaks between 20,000 and 25,000 feet.

Princesses: Were given to neighboring tribes to promote peace for China and commerce for the receiving country or tribe.

Raw onions: A folk remedy for healing used across most of Central Asia.

Sandstorms: Most common in the spring, the fine sand is carried eastward on the wind across China, Korea, Japan, the ocean, and often into North America. Current newspapers in Asia will warn of "yellow sand" days.

Turpan (ancient name was Gushi): Turpan is located in the Tarin basin—a region in the far northwest of China between the Tian Shan and Kunlun mountains. It is also the area where the Gobi Desert (gravel) to its east meets the Taklamakan Desert (sand) to its west. It is the second lowest and hottest place in the world after the Dead Sea. Famous for grapes and Hami melons, both grown along the oasis rivers.

Villagers speaking out at the trial: Entire villages went to listen to the trials. Chinese literature and movies show events like this where crowds participate in the trial and verdict with commentary, agreement, or objection.

Poems

My family married me to the other side of Heaven
and entrusted me in a foreign country
to be married to the King of Wusun.
The yurt is my house and felt is my walls.
Meat is my food and sour milk is my drink.
Living here, I am always longing for native soil,
wishing to turn into a yellow crane
and fly back home.

Princess Liu Xijun, ca. 105 BCE

Drege, Jean Pierre. *The Silk Road Saga*.
New York. Facts on File, 1989, p.10.

Originally I was a child of the Royal Household,
now darting around the camp of the barbarians
seeing both success and failure,
the emotion in my heart is unrestrained.
It's the same from ancient times,
I am not alone in my complaint.

Princess Chioen Chi, 528 CE

Elisabeth Benard, editor. *Goddesses Who Rule*.
New York. Oxford University Press, 2000, p. 153.

Biography

Hildi Kang is a former educator, a writer, and active traveler, having made trips by foot, bike, and llama. An early love of books and maps led to Hildi's dreams of the blue-domed mosques of Samarkand and the donkey market in Kashgar. In the 1990s, the Soviet-era barriers to travel fell, and Hildi, her husband, and two companions (plus driver and interpreter), spent a month following the trade routes around the Taklamakan desert in the northwest province of China and crossing into Uzbekistan to follow the road from the cities of Khiva to Samarkand.

At one point, as they drove eight hours on the one and only paved road between Khiva and Bukhara with nothing at all in sight except flat, barren, desolate land, Hildi vividly imagined a camel caravan making the same trip. The realization suddenly hit her that the "trade routes" are still in use: camel caravans have become truck caravans using the same but recently paved road, and travel is still in groups, for the dangers haven't changed. Photos preserve the trip; the story of Chengli shares it.

Closer to home, Hildi Kang is a graduate of the University of California, Berkeley, and as an educator, she taught elementary Special Education. Her writing includes five books for elementary school teachers, an entry in *Fire and Wings*, the dragon anthology of Cricket Books, and two academic books on Korean history.

When not writing or traveling, she hikes, bikes, and plays cello in a local orchestra. She and her family lived many years in the town of Clarence Center near Buffalo, New York, and currently reside in Livermore, California.